Joseph Sheridan Le Fanu

A Stable for nightmares; Weird tales

Joseph Sheridan Le Fanu

A Stable for nightmares; Weird tales

ISBN/EAN: 9783337024116

Printed in Europe, USA, Canada, Australia, Japan

Cover: Foto ©Andreas Hilbeck / pixelio.de

More available books at **www.hansebooks.com**

A STABLE FOR NIGHTMARES

A STABLE ❧ ❧ ❧ ❧
FOR NIGHTMARES

OR

WEIRD TALES

BY

J. SHERIDAN LE FANU
AUTHOR OF "UNCLE SILAS," "HOUSE BY THE CHURCHYARD,"

SIR CHARLES YOUNG, Bart.
AND OTHERS

Illustrated

NEW YORK
NEW AMSTERDAM BOOK COMPANY
156 FIFTH AVENUE
1896

TABLE OF CONTENTS

DICKON THE DEVIL.

DICKON THE DEVIL.

ABOUT thirty years ago I was selected by two rich old maids to visit a property in that part of Lancashire which lies near the famous forest of Pendle, with which Mr. Ainsworth's "Lancashire Witches" has made us so pleasantly familiar. My business was to make partition of a small property, including a house and demesne to which they had, a long time before, succeeded as coheiresses.

The last forty miles of my journey I was obliged to post, chiefly by cross-roads, little known, and less frequented, and presenting scenery often extremely interesting and pretty. The picturesqueness of the landscape was enhanced by the season, the beginning of September, at which ·I was travelling.

I had never been in this part of the world before; I am told it is now a great deal less wild, and, consequently, less beautiful.

At the inn where I had stopped for a relay of horses and some dinner—for it was then past five o'clock—I found the host, a hale old fellow of five-and-sixty, as he told me, a man of easy and garrulous benevolence, willing to accommodate his guests with any amount of talk, which the slightest tap sufficed to set flowing, on any subject you pleased.

I was curious to learn something about Barwyke, which was the name of the demesne and house I was going to. As there was no inn within some miles of it, I had written to the steward to put me up there, the best way he could, for a night.

The host of the "Three Nuns," which was the sign under which he entertained wayfarers, had not a great deal to tell. It was twenty years, or more, since old Squire Bowes died, and no one had lived in the Hall ever since, except the gardener and his wife.

"Tom Wyndsour will be as old a man as myself; but he's a bit taller, and not so much in flesh, quite," said the fat innkeeper.

"But there were stories about the house," I repeated, "that, they said, prevented tenants from coming into it?"

"Old wives' tales; many years ago, that will be, sir; I forget 'em; I forget 'em all. Oh yes, there always will be, when a house is left so; foolish folk will always be talkin'; but I han't heard a word about it this twenty year."

It was vain trying to pump him; the old landlord of the "Three Nuns," for some reason, did not choose to tell tales of Barwyke Hall, if he really did, as I suspected, remember them.

I paid my reckoning, and resumed my journey, well pleased with the good cheer of that old-world inn, but a little disappointed.

We had been driving for more than an hour, when we began to cross a wild common; and I knew that, this passed, a quarter of an hour would bring me to the door of Barwyke Hall.

The peat and furze were pretty soon left behind;

we were again in the wooded scenery that I enjoyed so much, so entirely natural and pretty, and
so little disturbed by traffic of any kind. I was
looking from the chaise-window, and soon detected
the object of which, for some time, my eye had
been in search. Barwyke Hall was a large, quaint
house, of that cage-work fashion known as "black-
and-white," in which the bars and angles of an oak
framework contrast, black as ebony, with the
white plaster that overspreads the masonry built
into its interstices. This steep-roofed Elizabethan
house stood in the midst of park-like grounds of
no great extent, but rendered imposing by the
noble stature of the old trees that now cast their
lengthening shadows eastward over the sward,
from the declining sun.

The park-wall was gray with age, and in many
places laden with ivy. In deep gray shadow,
that contrasted with the dim fires of evening reflected on the foliage above it, in a gentle hollow,
stretched a lake that looked cold and black, and
seemed, as it were, to skulk from observation with
a guilty knowledge.

I had forgot that there was a lake at Barwyke;
but the moment this caught my eye, like the cold
polish of a snake in the shadow, my instinct
seemed to recognize something dangerous, and I
knew that the lake was connected, I could not remember how, with the story I had heard of this
place in my boyhood.

I drove up a grass-grown avenue, under the
boughs of these noble trees, whose foliage, dyed
in autumnal red and yellow, returned the beams of
the western sun gorgeously.

We drew up at the door. I got out, and had a good look at the front of the house; it was a large and melancholy mansion, with signs of long neglect upon it; great wooden shutters, in the old fashion, were barred, outside, across the windows; grass, and even nettles, were growing thick on the court-yard, and a thin moss streaked the timber beams; the plaster was discolored by time and weather, and bore great russet and yellow stains. The gloom was increased by several grand old trees that crowded close about the house.

I mounted the steps, and looked round; the dark lake lay near me now, a little to the left. It was not large; it may have covered some ten or twelve acres; but it added to the melancholy of the scene. Near the centre of it was a small island, with two old ash-trees, leaning toward each other, their pensive images reflected in the stirless water. The only cheery influence of this scene of antiquity, solitude, and neglect was that the house and landscape were warmed with the ruddy western beams. I knocked, and my summons resounded hollow and ungenial in my ear; and the bell, from far away, returned a deep-mouthed and surly ring, as if it resented being roused from a score years' slumber.

A light-limbed, jolly-looking old fellow, in a barracan jacket and gaiters, with a smirk of welcome, and a very sharp, red nose, that seemed to promise good cheer, opened the door with a promptitude that indicated a hospitable expectation of my arrival.

There was but little light in the hall, and that little lost itself in darkness in the background. It

was very spacious and lofty, with a gallery running round it, which, when the door was open,
was visible at two or three points. Almost in the
dark my new acquaintance led me across this wide
hall into the room destined for my reception. It
was spacious, and wainscoted up to the ceiling.
The furniture of this capacious chamber was old-
fashioned and clumsy. There were curtains still
to the windows, and a piece of Turkey carpet lay
upon the floor; those windows were two in number, looking out, through the trunks of the trees
close to the house, upon the lake. It needed all
the fire, and all the pleasant associations of my
entertainer's red nose, to light up this melancholy
chamber. A door at its farther end admitted to
the room that was prepared for my sleeping apartment. It was wainscoted, like the other. It had
a four-post bed, with heavy tapestry curtains, and
in other respects was furnished in the same old-
world and ponderous style as the other room. Its
window, like those of that apartment, looked out
upon the lake.

Sombre and sad as these rooms were, they were
yet scrupulously clean. I had nothing to complain
of; but the effect was rather dispiriting. Having
given some directions about supper—a pleasant
incident to look forward to—and made a rapid
toilet, I called on my friend with the gaiters and
red nose (Tom Wyndsour), whose occupation was
that of a "bailiff," or under-steward, of the property, to accompany me, as we had still an hour
or so of sun and twilight, in a walk over the
grounds.

It was a sweet autumn evening, and my guide,

a hardy old fellow, strode at a pace that tasked me to keep up with.

Among clumps of trees at the northern boundary of the demesne we lighted upon the little antique parish church. I was looking down upon it, from an eminence, and the park-wall interposed; but a little way down was a stile affording access to the road, and by this we approached the iron gate of the churchyard. I saw the church door open; the sexton was replacing his pick, shovel, and spade, with which he had just been digging a grave in the churchyard, in their little repository under the stone stair of the tower. He was a polite, shrewd little hunchback, who was very happy to show me over the church. Among the monuments was one that interested me; it was erected to commemorate the very Squire Bowes from whom my two old maids had inherited the house and estate of Barwyke. It spoke of him in terms of grandiloquent eulogy, and informed the Christian reader that he had died, in the bosom of the Church of England, at the age of seventy-one.

I read this inscription by the parting beams of the setting sun, which disappeared behind the horizon just as we passed out from under the porch.

"Twenty years since the Squire died," said I, reflecting, as I loitered still in the churchyard.

"Ay, sir; 'twill be twenty year the ninth o' last month."

"And a very good old gentleman?"

"Good-natured enough, and an easy gentleman he was, sir; I don't think while he lived he ever hurt a fly," acquiesced Tom Wyndsour. "It ain't always easy sayin' what's in 'em, though, and what they may take or turn to afterward; and some o' them sort, I think, goes mad."

"You don't think he was out of his mind?" I asked.

"He? La! no; not he, sir; a bit lazy, may- hap, like other old fellows; but a knew devilish well what he was about."

Tom Wyndsour's account was a little enigmati- cal; but, like old Squire Bowes, I was "a bit lazy" that evening, and asked no more questions about him.

We got over the stile upon the narrow road that skirts the churchyard. It is overhung by elms more than a hundred years old, and in the twi- light, which now prevailed, was growing very dark. As side-by-side we walked along this road, hemmed in by two loose stone-like walls, some- thing running toward us in a zig-zag line passed us at a wild pace, with a sound like a frightened laugh or a shudder, and I saw, as it passed, that it was a human figure. I may confess, now, that I was a little startled. The dress of this figure was, in part, white: I know I mistook it at first for a white horse coming down the road at a gal- lop. Tom Wyndsour turned about and looked after the retreating figure.

"He'll be on his travels to-night," he said, in a low tone. "Easy served with a bed, *that* lad be; six foot o' dry peat or heath, or a nook in a dry ditch. That lad hasn't slept once in a house this twenty year, and never will while grass grows."

"Is he mad?" I asked.

"Something that way, sir; he's an idiot, an

awpy; we call him 'Dickon the devil,' because the devil's almost the only word that's ever in his mouth."

It struck me that this idiot was in some way connected with the story of old Squire Bowes.

"Queer things are told of him, I dare say?" I suggested.

"More or less, sir; more or less. Queer stories, some."

"Twenty years since he slept in a house? That's about the time the Squire died," I continued.

"So it will be, sir; not very long after."

"You must tell me all about that, Tom, to-night, when I can hear it comfortably, after supper."

Tom did not seem to like my invitation; and looking straight before him as we trudged on, he said:

"You see, sir, the house has been quiet, and nout's been troubling folk inside the walls or out, all round the woods of Barwyke, this ten year, or more; and my old woman, down there, is clear against talking about such matters, and thinks it best—and so do I—to let sleepin' dogs be."

He dropped his voice toward the close of the sentence, and nodded significantly.

We soon reached a point where he unlocked a wicket in the park wall, by which we entered the grounds of Barwyke once more.

The twilight deepening over the landscape, the huge and solemn trees, and the distant outline of the haunted house, exercised a sombre influence on me, which, together with the fatigue of a day of travel, and the brisk walk we had had, disinclined me to interrupt the silence in which my companion now indulged.

A certain air of comparative comfort, on our arrival, in great measure dissipated the gloom that was stealing over me. Although it was by no means a cold night, I was very glad to see some wood blazing in the grate; and a pair of candles aiding the light of the fire, made the room look cheerful. A small table, with a very white cloth, and preparations for supper, was also a very agreeable object.

I should have liked very well, under these influences, to have listened to Tom Wyndsour's story; but after supper I grew too sleepy to attempt to lead him to the subject; and after yawning for a time, I found there was no use in contending against my drowsiness, so I betook myself to my bedroom, and by ten o'clock was fast asleep.

What interruption I experienced that night I shall tell you presently. It was not much, but it was very odd.

By next night I had completed my work at Barwyke. From early morning till then I was so incessantly occupied and hard-worked, that I had no time to think over the singular occurrence to which I have just referred. Behold me, however, at length once more seated at my little supper-table, having ended a comfortable meal. It had been a sultry day, and I had thrown one of the large windows up as high as it would go. I was sitting near it, with my brandy and water at my elbow, looking out into the dark. There was no moon, and the trees that are grouped about the house make the darkness round it supernaturally profound on such nights.

"Tom," said I, so soon as the jug of hot punch

2

I had supplied him with began to exercise its genial and communicative influence; "you must tell
me who beside your wife and you and myself slept
in the house last night."

Tom, sitting near the door, set down his tum-
bler, and looked at me askance, while you might
count seven, without speaking a word.

"Who else slept in the house?" he repeated,
very deliberately. "Not a living soul, sir;" and
he looked hard at me, still evidently expecting
something more.   :

"That *is* very odd," I said, returning his stare,
and feeling really a little odd. "You are sure *you*
were not in my room last night?"

"Not till I came to call you, sir, this morning;
I can make oath of that."

"Well," said I, "there was some one there, *I*
can make oath of that. I was so tired I could not
make up my mind to get up; but I was waked by
a sound that I thought was some one flinging down
the two tin boxes in which my papers were locked
up violently on the floor. I heard a slow step on
the ground, and there was light in the room, although I remembered having put out my candle.
I thought it must have been you, who had come in
for my clothes, and upset the boxes by accident.
Whoever it was, he went out, and the light with
him. I was about to settle again, when, the curtain being a little open at the foot of the bed, I
saw a light on the wall opposite; such as a candle
from outside would cast if the door were very cautiously opening. I started up in the bed, drew
the side curtain, and saw that the door *was* opening, and admitting light from outside. It is close,

you know, to the head of the bed. A hand was holding on the edge of the door and pushing it open; not a bit like yours; a very singular hand. Let me look at yours."

He extended it for my inspection.

"Oh no; there's nothing wrong with your hand. This was differently shaped; fatter; and the middle finger was stunted, and shorter than the rest, looking as if it had once been broken, and the nail was crooked like a claw. I called out, "Who's there?" and the light and the hand were withdrawn, and I saw and heard no more of my visitor."

"So sure as you're a living man, that was him!" exclaimed Tom Wyndsour, his very nose growing pale, and his eyes almost starting out of his head.

"Who?" I asked.

"Old Squire Bowes; 'twas *his* hand you saw; the Lord a' mercy on us!" answered Tom. "The broken finger, and the nail bent like a hoop. Well for you, sir, he didn't come back when you called, that time. You came here about them Miss Dymock's business, and he never meant they should have a foot o' ground in Barwyke; and he was making a will to give it away quite different, when death took him short. He never was uncivil to no one; but he couldn't abide them ladies. My mind misgave me when I heard 'twas about their business you were coming; and now you see how it is; he'll be at his old tricks again!"

With some pressure, and a little more punch, I induced Tom Wyndsour to explain his mysterious allusions by recounting the occurrences which followed the old Squire's death.

"Squire Bowes, of Barwyke, died without mak‑
ing a will, as you know," said Tom. "And all
the folk round were sorry; that is to say, sir, as
sorry as folk will be for an old man that has seen
a long tale of years, and has no right to grumble
that death has knocked an hour too soon at his
door. The Squire was well liked; he was never
in a passion, or said a hard word; and he would
not hurt a fly; and that made what happened after
his decease the more surprising.

"The first thing these ladies did, when they got
the property, was to buy stock for the park.

"It was not wise, in any case, to graze the land
on their own account. But they little knew all
they had to contend with.

"Before long something went wrong with the
cattle; first one, and then another, took sick and
died, and so on, till the loss began to grow heavy.
Then, queer stories, little by little, began to be
told. It was said, first by one, then by another,
that Squire Bowes was seen, about evening time,
walking, just as he used to do when he was alive,
among the old trees, leaning on his stick; and,
sometimes, when he came up with the cattle, he
would stop and lay his hand kindly like on the
back of one of them; and that one was sure to fall
sick next day, and die soon after.

"No one ever met him in the park, or in the
woods, or ever saw him, except a good distance
off. But they knew his gait and his figure well,
and the clothes he used to wear; and they could
tell the beast he laid his hand on by its color—
white, dun, or black; and that beast was sure to
sicken and die. The neighbors grew shy of tak‑

ing the path over the park; and no one liked to walk in the woods, or come inside the bounds of Barwyke; and the cattle went on sickening and dying, as before.

"At that time there was one Thomas Pyke; he had been a groom to the old Squire; and he was in care of the place, and was the only one that used to sleep in the house.

"Tom was vexed, hearing these stories; which he did not believe the half on 'em; and more especial as he could not get man or boy to herd the cattle; all being afeared. So he wrote to Matlock, in Derybshire, for his brother, Richard Pyke, a clever lad, and one that knew nout o' the story of the old Squire walking.

"Dick came; and the cattle was better; folk said they could still see the old Squire, sometimes, walking, as before, in openings of the wood, with his stick in his hand; but he was shy of coming nigh the cattle, whatever his reason might be, since Dickon Pyke came; and he used to stand a long bit off, looking at them, with no more stir in him than a trunk o' one of the old trees, for an hour at a time, till the shape melted away, little by little, like the smoke of a fire that burns out.

"Tom Pyke and his brother Dickon, being the only living souls in the house, lay in the big bed in the servants' room, the house being fast barred and locked, one night in November.

"Tom was lying next the wall, and, he told me, as wide awake as ever he was at noonday. His brother Dickon lay outside, and was sound asleep.

"Well, as Tom lay thinking, with his eyes turned toward the door, it opens slowly, and who should come in but old Squire Bowes, his face lookin' as dead as he was in his coffin.

"Tom's very breath left his body; he could not take his eyes off him; and he felt their hair rising up on his head.

"The Squire came to the side of the bed, and put his arms under Dickon, and lifted the boy—in a dead sleep all the time—and carried him out so, at the door.

"Such was the appearance, to Tom Pyke's eyes, and he was ready to swear to it, anywhere.

"When this happened, the light, wherever it came from, all on a sudden went out, and Tom could not see his own hand before him.

"More dead than alive, he lay till daylight.

"Sure enough his brother Dickon was gone. No sign of him could he discover about the house; and with some trouble he got a couple of the neighbors to help him to search the woods and grounds. Not a sign of him anywhere.

"At last one of them thought of the island in the lake; the little boat was moored to the old post at the water's edge. In they got, though with small hope of finding him there. Find him, nevertheless, they did, sitting under the big ash-tree, quite out of his wits; and to all their questions he answered nothing but one cry—'Bowes, the devil! See him; see him; Bowes, the devil!' An idiot they found him; and so he will be till God sets all things right. No one could ever get him to sleep under roof-tree more. He wanders from house to house while daylight lasts; and no one cares to lock the harmless creature in the workhouse. And folk would rather not meet him after nightfall, for they think where he is there may be worse things near."

A silence followed Tom's story. He and I were alone in that large room; I was sitting near the open window, looking into the dark night air. I fancied I saw something white move across it; and I heard a sound like low talking, that swelled into a discordant shriek—"Hoo-oo-oo! Bowes, the devil! Over your shoulder. Hoo-oo-oo! ha! ha! ha!" I started up, and saw, by the light of the candle with which Tom strode to the window, the wild eyes and blighted face of the idiot, as, with a sudden change of mood, he drew off, whispering and tittering to himself, and holding up his long fingers, and looking at them as if they were lighted at the tips like a "hand of glory."

Tom pulled down the window. The story and its epilogue were over. I confessed I was rather glad when I heard the sound of the horses' hoofs on the courtyard, a few minutes later; and still gladder when, having bidden Tom a kind farewell, I had left the neglected house of Barwyke a mile behind me.

A DEBT OF HONOR.

A DEBT OF HONOR.

A GHOST STORY.

HUSH! what was that cry, so low but yet so piercing, so strange but yet so sorrowful? It was not the marmot upon the side of the Righi—it was not the heron down by the lake; no, it was distinctively human. Hush! there it is again —from the churchyard which I have just left!

Not ten minutes have elapsed since I was sitting on the low wall of the churchyard of Weggis, watching the calm glories of the moonlight illuminating with silver splendor the lake of Lucerne; and I am certain there was no one within the inclosure but myself.

I am mistaken, surely. What a silence there is upon the night! Not a breath of air now to break up into a thousand brilliant ripples the long reflection of the August moon, or to stir the foliage of the chestnuts; not a voice in the village; no splash of oar upon the lake. All life seems at perfect rest, and the solemn stillness that reigns about the topmost glaciers of S. Gothard has spread its mantle over the warmer world below.

I must not linger; as it is, I shall have to wake up the porter to let me into the hotel. I hurry on.

Not ten paces, though. Again I hear the cry.

This time it sounds to me like the long, sad sob of
a wearied and broken heart.   Without staying
to reason with myself, I quickly retrace my
steps.

I stumble about among the iron crosses and the
graves, and displace in my confusion wreaths of
immortelles and fresher flowers.   A huge mausoleum stands between me and the wall upon which
I had been sitting not a quarter of an hour ago.
The mausoleum casts a deep shadow upon the side
nearest to me.   Ah! something is stirring there.
I strain my eyes—the figure of a man passes slowly
out of the shade, and silently occupies my place
upon the wall.   It must have been his lips that
gave out that miserable sound.

What shall I do?   Compassion and curiosity are
strong.   The man whose heart can be rent so
sorely ought not to be allowed to linger here with
his despair.   He is gazing, as I did, upon the lake.
I mark his profile—clear-cut and symmetrical; I
catch the lustre of large eyes.   The face, as I can
see it, seems very still and placid.   I may be mistaken; he may merely be a wanderer like myself;
perhaps he heard the three strange cries, and has
also come to seek the cause.   I feel impelled to
speak to him.

I pass from the path by the church to the east
side of the mausoleum, and so come toward him,
the moon full upon his features.   Great heaven!
how pale his face is!   •   ·

"Good-evening, sir.   I thought myself alone
here, and wondered that no other travellers had
found their way to this lovely spot.   Charming, is
it not?"

For a moment he says nothing, but his eyes are full upon me. At last he replies:

"It is charming, as you say, Mr. Reginald Westcar."

"You know me?" I exclaim, in astonishment.

"Pardon me, I can scarcely claim a personal acquaintance. But yours is the only English name entered to-day in the Livre des Étrangers."

"You are staying at the Hôtel de la Concorde, then?"

An inclination of the head is all the answer vouchsafed.

"May I ask," I continue, "whether you heard just now a very strange cry repeated three times?"

A pause. The lustrous eyes seem to search me through and through—I can hardly bear their gaze. Then he replies.

"I fancy I heard the echoes of some such sounds as you describe."

The *echoes!* Is this, then, the man who gave utterance to those cries of woe! is it possible? The face seems so passionless; but the pallor of those features bears witness to some terrible agony within.

"I thought some one must be in distress," I rejoin, hastily; "and I hurried back to see if I could be of any service."

"Very good of you," he answers, coldly; "but surely such a place as this is not unaccustomed to the voice of sorrow."

"No doubt. My impulse was a mistaken one."

"But kindly meant. You will not sleep less soundly for acting on that impulse, Reginald Westcar."

He rises as he speaks. He throws his cloak round him, and stands motionless. I take the hint. My mysterious countryman wishes to be alone. Some one that he has loved and lost lies buried here.

"Good-night, sir," I say, as I move in the direction of the little chapel at the gate. "Neither of us will sleep the less soundly for thinking of the perfect repose that reigns around this place."

"What do you mean?" he asks.

"The dead," I reply, as I stretch my hand toward the graves. "Do you not remember the lines in 'King Lear'?

"'After life's fitful fever he sleeps well.'"

"But *you* have never died, Reginald Westcar. You know nothing of the sleep of death."

For the third time he speaks my name almost familiarly, and—I know not why—a shudder passes through me. I have no time, in my turn, to ask him what he means; for he strides silently away into the shadow of the church, and I, with a strange sense of oppression upon me, returned to my hotel.

The events which I have just related passed in vivid recollection through my mind as I travelled northward one cold November day in the year 185-. About six months previously I had taken my degree at Oxford, and had since been enjoying a trip upon the continent; and on my return to London I found a letter awaiting me from my lawyers, informing me somewhat to my astonishment, that I had succeeded to a small estate in Cumberland. I must tell you exactly how this came about. My mother was a Miss Ringwood, and she was the youngest of three children: the eldest was Aldina, the second was Geoffrey, and the third (my mother) Alice. Their mother (who had been a widow since my mother's birth) lived at this little place in Cumberland, and which was known as The Shallows; she died shortly after my mother's marriage with my father, Captain Westcar. My aunt Aldina and my uncle Geoffrey—the one at that time aged twenty-eight, and the other twenty-six—continued to reside at The Shallows. My father and mother had to go to India, where I was born, and where, when quite a child, I was left an orphan. A few months after my mother's marriage my aunt disappeared; a few weeks after that event, and my uncle Geoffrey dropped down dead, as he was playing at cards with Mr. Maryon, the proprietor of a neighboring mansion known as The Mere. A fortnight after my uncle's death, my aunt Aldina returned to The Shallows, and never left it again till she was carried out in her coffin to her grave in the churchyard. Ever since her return from her mysterious disappearance she maintained an impenetrable reserve. As a schoolboy I visited her twice or thrice, but these visits depressed my youthful spirits to such an extent, that as I grew older I excused myself from accepting my aunt's not very pressing invitations; and at the time I am now speaking of I had not seen her for eight or ten years. I was rather surprised, therefore, when she bequeathed me The Shallows, which, as the surviving child, she inherited under her mother's marriage settlement.

But The Shallows had always exercised a grim influence over me, and the knowledge that I was now going to it as my home oppressed me. The road seemed unusually dark, cold, and lonely. At last I passed the lodge, and two hundred yards more brought me to the porch. Very soon the door was opened by an elderly female, whom I well remembered as having been my aunt's housekeeper and cook. I had pleasant recollections of her, and was glad to see her. To tell the truth, I had not anticipated my visit to my newly acquired property with any great degree of enthusiasm; but a very tolerable dinner had an inspiriting effect, and I was pleased to learn that there was a bin of old Madeira in the cellar. Naturally I soon grew cheerful, and consequently talkative; and summoned Mrs. Balk for a little gossip. The substance of what I gathered from her rather diffusive conversation was as follows:

My aunt had resided at The Shallows ever since the death of my uncle Geoffrey, but she had maintained a silent and reserved habit; and Mrs. Balk was of opinion that she had had some great misfortune. She had persistently refused all intercourse with the people at The Mere. Squire Maryon, himself a cold and taciturn man, had once or twice showed a disposition to be friendly, but she had sternly repulsed all such overtures. Mrs. Balk was of opinion that Miss Ringwood was not "quite right," as she expressed it, on some topics; especially did she seem impressed with the idea that The Mere ought to belong to her. It

appeared that the Ringwoods and Maryons were
distant connections; that The Mere belonged in
former times to a certain Sir Henry Benet; that
he was a bachelor, and that Squire Maryon's father
and old Mr. Ringwood were cousins of his, and
that there was some doubt as to which was the
real heir; that Sir Henry, who disliked old Maryon, had frequently said he had set any chance of
dispute at rest, by bequeathing the Mere property
by will to Mr. Ringwood, my mother's father;
that, on his death, no such will could be found;
and the family lawyers agreed that Mr. Maryon
was the legal inheritor, and my uncle Geoffrey and
his sisters must be content to take the Shallows,
or nothing at all. Mr. Maryon was comparatively
rich, and the Ringwoods poor, consequently they
were advised not to enter upon a costly lawsuit.
My aunt Aldina maintained to the last that Sir
Henry had made a will, and that Mr. Maryon
knew it, but had destroyed or suppressed the document. I did not gather from Mrs. Balk's narrative
that Miss Ringwood had any foundation for her belief, and I dismissed the notion at once as baseless.

"And my uncle Geoffrey died of apoplexy, you
say, Mrs. Balk?"

"*I* don't say so, sir, no more did Miss Ringwood; but *they* said so."

"Whom do you mean by *they?*"

"The people at The Mere—the young doctor, a
friend of Squire Maryon's, who was brought over
from York, and the rest; he fell heavily from his
chair, and his head struck against the fender."

"Playing at cards with Mr. Maryon, I think
you said."

3

"Yes, sir; he was too fond of cards, I believe,
was Mr. Geoffrey."

"Is Mr. Maryon seen much in the county—is he
hospitable?"

"Well, sir, he goes up to London a good deal,
and has some friends down from town occasionally;
but he does not seem to care much about the people in the neighborhood."

"He has some children, Mrs. Balk?"

"Only one daughter, sir; a sweet pretty thing
she is. Her mother died when Miss Agnes was
born."

"You have no idea, Mrs. Balk, what my aunt
Aldina's great misfortune was?"

"Well, sir, I can't help thinking it must have
been a love affair. She always hated men so
much."

"Then why did she leave The Shallows to me,
Mrs. Balk?"

"Ah, you are laughing, sir. No doubt she considered that The Mere ought to belong to you, as
the heir of the Ringwoods, and she placed you
here, as near as might be to the place."

"In hopes that I might marry Miss Maryon, eh,
Mrs. Balk?"

"You are laughing again, sir. I don't imagine
she thought so much of that, as of the possibility
of your discovering something about the missing
will."

I bade the communicative Mrs. Balk good night
and retired to my bedroom—a low, wide, sombre,
oak-panelled chamber. I must confess that family stories had no great interest for me, living
apart from them at school and college as I had

done; and as I undressed I thought more of the
probabilities of sport the eight hundred acres of
wild shooting belonging to The Shallows would
afford me, than of the supposed will my poor aunt
had evidently worried herself about so much.
Thoroughly tired after my long journey, I soon
fell fast asleep amid the deep shadows of the huge
four-poster I mentally resolved to chop up into
firewood at an early date, and substitute for it a
more modern iron bedstead.

How long I had been asleep I do not know, but
I suddenly started up, the echo of a long, sad cry
ringing in my ears.

I listened eagerly—sensitive to the slightest
sound—painfully sensitive as one is only in the
deep silence of the night.

I heard the old-fashioned clock I had noticed on
the stairs strike three. The reverberation seemed
to last a long time, then all was silent again. "A
dream," I muttered to myself, as I lay down upon
the pillow; "Madeira is a heating wine. But
what can I have been dreaming of?"

Sleep seemed to have gone altogether, and the
busy mind wandered among the continental scenes
I had lately visited. By and by I found myself
in memory once more within the Weggis churchyard. I was satisfied; I had traced my dream to
the cries that I had heard there. I turned round
to sleep again. Perhaps I fell into a doze—I cannot say; but again I started up at the repetition,
as it seemed outside my window, of that cry of
sadness and despair. I hastily drew aside the
heavy curtains of my bed—at that moment the
room seemed to be illuminated with a dim, un-

earthly light—and I saw, gradually growing into
human shape, the figure of a woman. I recognized in it my aunt, Miss Ringwood. Horror-
struck, I gazed at the apparition; it advanced
a little—the lips moved—I heard it distinctly
say:

"*Reginald Westcar, The Mere belongs to you.
Compel John Maryon to pay the debt of honor!*"

I fell back senseless.

When next I returned to consciousness, it was
when I was called in the morning; the shutters
were opened, and I saw the red light of the dawn-
ing winter sun.

There is a strange sympathy between the night
and the mind. All one's troubles represent themselves as increased a hundredfold if one wakes in
the night, and begins to think about them. A
muscular pain becomes the certainty of an incur-
able internal disease; and a headache suggests incipient softening of the brain. But all these
horrors are dissipated with the morning light, and
the after-glow of a cold bath turns them into jokes.
So it was with me on the morning after my arrival
at The Shallows. I accounted most satisfactorily
for all that had occurred, or seemed to have occurred, during the night; and resolved that,
though the old Madeira was uncommonly good, I
must be careful in future not to drink more than a
couple of glasses after dinner. I need scarcely say
that I said nothing to Mrs. Balk of my bad dreams,
and shortly after breakfast I took my gun, and went
out in search of such game as I might chance to
meet with. At three o'clock I sent the keeper

home, as his capacious pockets were pretty well
filled, telling him that I thought I knew the country, and should stroll back leisurely. The gray
gloom of the November evening was spreading
over the sky as I came upon a small plantation
which I believed belonged to me. I struck straight
across it; emerging from its shadows, I found myself by a small stream and some marshy land; on
the other side another small plantation. A snipe
got up, I fired, and tailored it. I marked the bird
into this other plantation, and followed. Up got
a covey of partridges—bang, bang—one down by
the side of an oak. I was about to enter this cov-
ert, when a lady and gentleman emerged, and,
struck with the unpleasant thought that I was possibly trespassing, I at once went forward to apolo-
gize.

Before I could say a word, the gentleman addressed me.

"May I ask, sir, if I have given you permission
to shoot over my preserves?"

"I beg to express my great regret, sir," I replied, as I lifted my hat in acknowledgment of the
lady's presence, "that I should have trespassed
upon your land. I can only plead, as my excuse,
that I fully believed I was still upon the manor
belonging to The Shallows."

"Gentlemen who go out shooting ought to know
the limits of their estates," he answered harshly;
"the boundaries of The Shallows are well defined,
nor is the area they contain so very extensive.
You have no right upon this side the stream, sir;
oblige me by returning."

I merely bowed, for I was nettled by his tone,

and as I turned away I noticed that the young lady whispered to him.

"One moment, sir," he said, "my daughter suggests the possibility of your being the new owner of The Shallows. May I ask if this is so?"

It had not occurred to me before, but I understood in a moment to whom I had been speaking, and I replied:

"Yes, Mr. Maryon—my name is Westcar."

Such was my introduction to Mr. and Miss Maryon. The proprietor of The Mere appeared to be a gentleman, but his manners were cold and reserved, and a careful observer might have remarked a perpetual restlessness in the eyes, as if they were physically incapable of regarding the same object for more than a moment. He was about sixty years of age, apparently; and though he now and again made an effort to carry himself upright, the head and shoulders soon drooped again, as if the weight of years, and, it might be, the memory of the past, were a heavy load to carry. Of Miss Maryon it is sufficient to say that she was nineteen or twenty, and it did not need a second glance to satisfy me that her beauty was of no ordinary kind.

I must hurry over the records of the next few weeks. I became a frequent visitor at The Mere. Mr. Maryon's manner never became cordial, but he did not seem displeased to see me; and as to Agnes,—well, she certainly was not displeased either.

I think it was on Christmas Day that I suddenly discovered that I was desperately in love. Miss Maryon had been for two or three days confined to

her room by a bad cold, and I found myself in a
great state of anxiety to see her again. I am sorry
to say that my thoughts wandered a good deal
when I was at church upon that festival, and I
could not help thinking what ample room there
was for a bridal procession up the spacious aisle.
Suddenly my eyes rested upon a mural tablet, in-
scribed, "To the memory of Aldina Ringwood."
Then with a cold thrill there came back upon me
what I had almost forgotten, the dream, or whatever it was, that had occurred on that first night at
The Shallows; and those strange words—"The
Mere belongs to you. Compel John Maryon to
pay the debt of honor!" Nothing but the remembrance of Agnes' sweet face availed for the time
to banish the vision, the statement, and the bidding.

Miss Maryon was soon down-stairs again. Did
I flatter myself too much in thinking that she was
as glad to see me as I was to see her? No—I felt
sure that I did not. Then I began to reflect seriously upon my position. My fortune was small,
quite enough for me, but not enough for two; and
as she was heiress of The Mere and a comfortable
rent-roll of some six or eight thousand a year, was
it not natural that Mr. Maryon expected her to
make what is called a "good match"? Still, I could
not conceal from myself the fact, that he evinced
no objection whatever to my frequent visits at his
house, nor to my taking walks with his daughter
when he was unable to accompany us.

One bright, frosty day I had been down to the
lake with Miss Maryon, and had enjoyed the privi-
ilege of teaching her to skate; and on returning to
the house, we met Mr. Maryon upon the terrace,

He walked with us to the conservatory; we went
in to examine the plants, and he remained outside,
pacing up and down the terrace. Both Agnes and
myself were strangely silent; perhaps my tongue
had found an eloquence upon the ice which was
well met by a shy thoughtfulness upon her part.
But there was a lovely color upon her cheeks, and
I experienced a very considerable and unusual flut-
tering about my heart. It happened as we were
standing at the door of the conservatory, both of
us silently looking away from the flowers upon
the frosty view, that our eyes lighted at the same
time upon Mr. Maryon. He, too, was apparently
regarding the prospect, when suddenly he paused
and staggered back, as if something unexpected
met his gaze.

"Oh, poor papa! I hope he is not going to have
one of his fits!" exclaimed Agnes.

"Fits! Is he subject to such attacks?" I inquired.

"Not ordinary fits," she answered hurriedly;
"I hardly know how to explain them. They come
upon him occasionally, and generally at this period of the year."

"Shall we go to him?" I suggested.

"No; you cannot help him; and he cannot bear
that they should be noticed."

We both watched him. His arms were stretched
up above his head, and again he recoiled a step or
two. I sought for an explanation in Agnes' face.

"A stranger!" she exclaimed. "Who can it
be?"

I looked toward Mr. Maryon. A tall figure of
a man had come from the farther side of the house;

he wore a large, loose coat and a kind of military cap upon his head.

"Doubtless you are surprised to see me, John," we heard the new-comer say, in a confident voice, "but I am not the devil, man, that you should greet me with such a peculiar attitude." He held out his hand, and continued, "Come, don't let the warmth of old fellowship be all on one side, this wintry day."

We could see that Mr. Maryon took the proffered right hand with his left for an instant, then seemed to shrink away, but exchanged no word of this greeting.

"I don't understand this," said Agnes, and we both hurried forward. The stranger, seeing Agnes approach, lifted his cap.

"Ah, your daughter, John, no doubt. I see the likeness to her lamented mother. Pray introduce me."

Mr. Maryon's usually pallid features had assumed a still paler hue, and he said in a low voice:

"Colonel Bludyer—my daughter." Agnes barely bowed.

"Charmed to renew your acquaintance, Miss Maryon. When last I saw you, you were quite a baby; but your father and I are very old friends—are we not, John?"

Mr. Maryon vaguely nodded his head.

"Well, John, you have often pressed your hospitality upon me, but till now I have never had an opportunity of availing myself of your kind offers; so I have brought my bag, and intend at last to give you the pleasure of my company for a few days."

I certainly should have thought that a man of
Mr. Maryon's disposition would have resented
such conduct as this, or, at all events, have given
this self-invited guest a chilling welcome. Mr.
Maryon, however, in a confused and somewhat
stammering tone, said that he was glad Colonel
Bludyer had come at last, and bade his daughter
go and make the necessary arrangements. Agnes,
in silent astonishment, entered the house, and then
Mr. Maryon turned to me hastily and bade me
good-by. In a by no means comfortable frame of
mind I returned to The Shallows.

The sudden advent of this miscellaneous colonel
was naturally somewhat irritating to me. Not
only did I regard the man as an intolerable bore,
but I could not help fancying that he was something more than an old friend of Mr. Maryon's; in
fact, I was led to judge, by Mr. Maryon's strange
conduct, that this Bludyer had some power over
him which might be exercised to the detriment of
the Maryon family, and I was convinced there was
some mystery it was my business to penetrate.

The following day I went up to The Mere to see
if Miss Maryon was desirous of renewing her skat-
ing lesson. I found the party in the billiard-room,
Agnes marking for her father and the Colonel.
Mr. Maryon, whom I knew to be an exceptionally
good player, seemed incapable of making a decent
stroke; the Colonel, on the other hand, could evidently give a professional fifteen, and beat him
easily. We all went down to the lake together. I
had no chance of any quiet conversation with Agnes; the Colonel was perpetually beside us.

I returned home disgusted. For two whole days

I did not go near The Mere. On the third day I went up, hoping that the horrid Colonel would be gone. It was beginning to snow when I left The Shallows at about two o'clock in the afternoon, and Mrs. Balk foretold a heavy storm, and bade me not be late returning.

The black winter darkness in the sky deepened as I approached The Mere. I was ushered again into the billiard-room. Agnes was marking, as upon the previous occasion, but two days had worked a sad difference in her face. Mr. Maryon hardly noticed my entrance; he was flushed, and playing eagerly; the Colonel was boisterous, declaring that John had never played better twenty years ago. I relieved Agnes of the duty of marking. The snow fell in a thick layer upon the skylight, and the Colonel became seriously anxious about my return home. As I did not think he was the proper person to give me hints, I resolutely remained where I was, encouraged in my behavior by the few words I gained from Agnes, and by the looks of entreaty she gave me. I had always considered Mr. Maryon to be an abstemious man, but he drank a good deal of brandy and soda during the long game of seven hundred up, and when he succeeded in beating the Colonel by forty-three, he was in roaring spirits, and insisted upon my staying to dinner. Need I say that I accepted the invitation?

I made such toilet as I could in a most unattainable chamber that was allotted to me, and hurried back to the drawing-room in the hope that I might get a few private words with Agnes. I was not disappointed. She, too, had hurried

down, and in a few words I learned that this
abominable Bludyer was paying her his coarse
attentions, and with, apparently, the full consent
of Mr. Maryon. My indignation was unbounded.
Was it possible that Mr. Maryon intended to sacrifice this fair creature to that repulsive man?

Mr. Maryon had appeared in excellent spirits
when dinner began, and the first glass or two of
champagne made him merrier than I thought it
possible for him to be. But by the time the dessert was on the table he had grown silent and
thoughtful; nor did he respond to the warm eulo-
giums the Colonel passed upon the magnum of
claret which was set before us.

After dinner we sat in the library. The Colonel
left the room to fetch some cigars he had been
loudly extolling. Then Agnes had an opportunity
of whispering to me.

"Look at papa—see how strangely he sits—his
hands clenching the arms of the chair, his eyes
fixed upon the blazing coals! How old he seems
to be to-night! His terrible fits are coming on—
he is always like this toward the end of January!"
The Colonel's return put an end to any further
confidential talk.

When we separated for the night, I felt that my
going to bed would be purposeless. I felt most
painfully wide awake. I threw myself down upon
my bed, and worried myself by trying to imagine
what secret there could be between Maryon and
Bludyer—for that a secret of some kind existed, I
felt certain. I tossed about till I heard the stroke
of one. A dreadful restlessness had come upon
me. It seemed as if the solemn night-side of life

was busy waking now, but the silence and solitude
of my antique chamber became too much for me.
I rose from my bed, and paced up and down the
room. I raked up the dying embers of the fire,
and drew an arm-chair to the hearth. I fell into
a doze. By and by I woke up suddenly, and I
was conscious of stealthy footsteps in the passage.
My sense of hearing became painfully acute. I
heard the footsteps retreating down the corridor,
until they were lost in the distance. I cautiously
opened the door, and, shading the candle with my
hand, looked out—there was nothing to be seen;
but I felt that I could not remain quietly in my
room, and, closing the door behind me, I went out
in search of I knew not what.

The sitting-rooms and bedrooms in ordinary use
at The Mere were in the modern part of the house;
but there was an old Elizabethan wing which I had
often longed to explore, and in this strange ramble
of mine I soon had reason to be satisfied that I was
well within it. At the end of an oak-panelled
narrow passage a door stood open, and I entered a
low, sombre apartment fitted with furniture in the
style of two hundred years ago. There was something awfully ghostly about the look of this room.
A great four-post bedstead, with heavy hangings,
stood in a deep recess; a round oak table and two
high-backed chairs were in the centre of the room.
Suddenly, as I gazed on these things, I heard
stealthy footsteps in the passage, and saw a dim
light advancing. Acting on a sudden impulse, I
extinguished my candle and withdrew into the
shadow of the recess, watching eagerly. The footsteps came nearer. My heart seemed to stand still

with expectation. They paused outside the door,
for a moment really—for an age it seemed to me.
Then, to my astonishment, I saw Mr. Maryon
enter. He carried a small night-lamp in his hand.
Another glance satisfied me that he was walking in
his sleep. He came straight to the round table,
and set down the lamp. He seated himself in one
of the high-backed chairs, his vacant eyes staring
at the chair opposite; then his lips began to move
quickly, as if he were addressing some one. Then
he rose, went to the bureau, and seemed to take
something from it; then he sat down again. What
a strange action of his hands! At first I could not
understand it; then it flashed upon me that in this
dream of his he must be shuffling cards. Yes, he
began to deal; then he was playing with his adversary—his lips moving anxiously at times.

A look of terrible eagerness came over the sleep-
walker's countenance. With nimble fingers he
dealt the cards, and played. Suddenly with a
sweep of his hand he seemed to fling the pack into
the fireplace, started from his seat, grappled with
his unseen adversary, raised his powerful right
hand, and struck a tremendous blow. Hush!
more footsteps along the passage! Am I de-
ceived? From my concealment I watch for what
is to follow. Colonel Bludyer comes in, half
dressed, but wide awake.

"You maniac!" I hear him mutter: "I expected
you were given to such tricks as these. Lucky for
you no eyes but mine have seen your abject folly.
Come baack to your room."

Mr. Maryon is still gazing, his arms lifted wildly
above his head, upon the imagined foe whom he

had felled to the ground. The Colonel touches
him on the shoulder, and leads him away, leaving
the lamp. My reasoning faculties had fully returned to me. I held a clue to the secret, and for
Agnes' sake it must be followed up. I took the
lamp away, and placed it on a table where the
chamber candlesticks stood, relit my own candle,
and found my way back to my bedroom.

The next morning, when I came down to breakfast, I found Colonel Bludyer warming himself
satisfactorily at the blazing fire. I learned from
him that our host was far from well, and that Miss
Maryon was in attendance upon her father; that
the Colonel was charged with all kinds of apologies
to me, and good wishes for my safe return home
across the snow. I thanked him for the delivery
of the message, while I felt perfectly convinced
that he had never been charged with it. However
that might be, I never saw Mr. Maryon that morning; and I started back to The Shallows through
the snow.

For the next two or three days the weather was
very wild, but I contrived to get up to The Mere,
and ask after Mr. Maryon. Better, I was told,
but unable to see any one. Miss Maryon, too, was
fatigued with nursing her father. So there was
nothing to do but to trudge home again.

"*Reginald Westcar, The Mere is yours. Compel John Maryon to pay the debt of honor!*"
Again and again these words forced themselves
upon me, as I listlessly gazed out upon the white
landscape. The strange scene that I had witnessed
on that memorable night I passed beneath Mr.
Maryon's roof had brought them back to my mem-

ory with redoubled force, and I began to think that the apparition I had seen—or dreamed of—on my first night at The Shallows had more of truth in it than I had been willing to believe.

Three more days passed away, and a carter-boy from The Mere brought me a note. It was Agnes' handwriting. It said:

DEAR MR. WESTCAR: Pray come up here, if you possibly can. I cannot understand what is the matter with papa; and he wishes me to do a dreadful thing. Do come. I feel that I have no friend but you. I am obliged to send this note privately."

I need scarcely say that five minutes afterward I was plunging through the snow toward The Mere. It was already late on that dark February evening as I gained the shrubbery; and as I was pondering upon the best method of securing admittance, I became aware that the figure of a man was hurrying on some yards in front of me. At first I thought it must be one of the gardeners, but all of a sudden I stood still, and my blood seemed to freeze with horror, as I remarked that the figure in front of me *left no trace of footmarks on the snow!* My brain reeled for a moment, and I thought I should have fallen; but I recovered my nerves, and when I looked before me again, it had disappeared. I pressed on eagerly. I arrived at the front door—it was wide open; and I passed through the hall to the library. I heard Agnes' voice.

"No, no, papa. You must not force me to this! I cannot—will not—marry Colonel Bludyer!"

"You *must*," answered Mr. Maryon, in a hoarse voice; "you *must* marry him, and save your father from something worse than disgrace!"

Not feeling disposed to play the eavesdropper, I entered the room. Mr. Maryon was standing at the fireplace. Agnes was crouching on the ground at his feet. I saw at once that it was no use for me to dissemble the reason of my visit, and, without a word of greeting, I said:

"Miss Maryon, I have come, in obedience to your summons. If I can prevent any misfortune from falling upon you I am ready to help you, with my life. You have guessed that I love you. If my love is returned I am prepared to dispute my claim with any man."

Agnes, with a cry of joy, rose from her knees, and rushed toward me. Ah! how strong I felt as I held her in my arms!

"I have my answer," I continued. "Mr. Maryon, I have reason to believe that your daughter is in fear of the future you have forecast for her. I ask you to regard those fears, and to give her to me, to love and cherish as my wife."

Mr. Maryon covered his face with his hands; and I could hear him murmur, "Too late—too late!"

"No, not too late," I echoed. "What is this Bludyer to you, that you should sacrifice your daughter to a man whose very look proclaims him a villain? Nothing can compel you to such a deed —not even *a debt of honor!*"

What it was impelled me to say these last words I know not, but they had an extraordinary effect upon Mr. Maryon. He started toward me, then checked himself; his face was livid, his eyeballs glaring, and he threw up his arms in the strange manner I had already witnessed.

4

"What is all this?" exclaimed a harsh voice behind me. "Mr. Westcar insulting Miss Maryon and her father! it is time for me to interfere." And Colonel Bludyer approached me menacingly. All his jovial manner and fulsome courtesy was gone; and in his flushed face and insolent look the savage rascal was revealed.

"You will interfere at your peril," I replied. "I am a younger man than you are, and my strength has not been weakened by drink and dissipation. Take care."

The villain drew himself up to his full height; and, though he must have been at least some sixty years of age, I felt assured that I should meet no ordinary adversary if a personal struggle should ensue. Agnes fainted, and I laid her on a sofa.

"Miss Maryon wants air," said the Colonel, in a calmer voice. "Excuse me, Mr. Maryon, if I open a window." He tore open the shutters, and threw up the sash. "And now, Mr. Westcar, unless you are prepared to be sensible, and make your exit by the door, I shall be under the unpleasant necessity of throwing you out of the window."

The ruffian advanced toward me as he spoke. Suddenly he paused. His jaw dropped; his hair seemed literally to stand on end; his white lips quivered; he shook, as with an ague; his whole form appeared to shrink. I stared in amazement at the awful change. A strange thrill shot through me, as I heard a quiet voice say:

"Richard Bludyer, your grave is waiting for you. Go."

The figure of a man passed between me and him.

The wretched man shrank back, and, with a wild cry, leaped from the window he had opened.

All this time Mr. Maryon was standing like a lifeless statue.

In helpless wonder I gazed at the figure before me. I saw clearly the features in profile, and, swift as lightning, my memory was carried back to the unforgotten scene in the churchyard upon the Lake of Lucerne, and I recognized the white face of the young man with whom I there had spoken.

"John Maryon," said the voice, "this is the night upon which, a quarter of a century ago, you killed me. It is your last night on earth. You must go through the tragedy again."

Mr. Maryon, still statue-like, beckoned to the figure, and opened a half-concealed door which led into his study. The strange but opportune visitant seemed to motion to me with a gesture of his hand, which I felt I must obey, and I followed in this weird procession. From the study we mounted by a private staircase to a large, well-furnished bed-chamber. Here we paused. Mr. Maryon looked tremblingly at the stranger, and said, in a low, stammering voice:

"This is my room. In this room, on this night, twenty-five years ago, you told me that you were certain Sir Henry Benet's will was in existence, and that you had made up your mind to dispute my possession to this property. You had discovered letters from Sir Henry to your father which gave you a clue to the spot where that will might be found. You, Geoffrey Ringwood, of generous and extravagant nature, offered to find the will in my presence. It was late at night, as now; all the household slept. I accepted your invitation, and followed you."

Mr. Maryon ceased; he seemed physically unable to continue. The terrible stranger, in his low, echoing voice, replied:

"Go on; confess all."

"You and I, Geoffrey,·had been what the world calls friends. We had been much in London together; we were both passionately fond of cards. We had a common acquaintance, Richard Bludyer. He was present on the 2d of February, when I lost a large sum of money to you at *écarté*. He hinted to me that you might possibly use these sums in instituting a lawsuit against me for the recovery of this estate. Your intimation that you knew of the existence of the will alarmed me, as it had become necessary for me to remain owner of The Mere. As I have said, I accepted your invitation, and followed you to Sir Henry Benet's room; and now I follow you again."

As he said these words, Geoffrey Ringwood, or his ghost, passed silently by Mr. Maryon, and led the way into the corridor. At the end of the corridor all three paused outside an oak door which I remembered well. A gesture from the leader made Mr. Maryon continue:

"On this threshold you told me suddenly that Bludyer was a villain, and had betrayed your sister Aldina; that she had fled with him that night; that he could never marry her, as you had reason to know he had a wife alive. You made me swear to help you in your vengeance against him. We entered the room, as we enter it now."

Our leader had opened the door of the room,

and we were in the same chamber I had wandered to when I had slept at The Mere. The figure of Geoffrey Ringwood paused at the round table, and looked again at Mr. Maryon, who proceeded:

"You went straight to the fifth panel from the fireplace, and then touched a spring, and the panel opened. You said that the will giving this property to your father and his heirs was to be found there. I was convinced that you spoke the truth, but, suddenly remembering your love of gambling, I suggested that we should play for it. You accepted at once. We searched among the papers, and found the will. We placed the will upon the table, and began to play. We agreed that we would play up to ten thousand pounds. Your luck was marvellous. In two hours the limit was reached. I owed you ten thousand pounds, and had lost The Mere. You laughed, and said, 'Well, John, you have had a fair chance. At ten o'clock this morning I shall expect you to pay me *your debt of honor.*' I rose; the devil of despair strong upon me. With one hand I swept the cards from the table into the fire, and with the other seized you by the throat, and dealt you a blow upon the temple. You fell dead upon the floor."

Need I say that as I heard this fearful narrative, I recognized the actions of the sleep-walker, and understood them all?

"To the end!" said the hollow voice. "Confess to the end!"

"The doctor who examined your body gave his opinion, at the inquest, that you had died of apoplexy, caused by strong cerebral excitement. My evidence was to the effect that I believed you had lost a very large sum of money to Captain Bludyer, and that you had told me you were utterly unable to pay it. The jury found their verdict accordingly, and I was left in undisturbed possession of The Mere. But the memory of my crime haunted me as only such memories can haunt a criminal, and I became a morose and miserable man. One thing bound me to life—my daughter. When Reginald Westcar appeared upon the scene I thought that the debt of honor would be satisfied if he married Agnes. Then Bludyer reappeared, and he told me that he knew that I had killed you. He threatened to revive the story, to exhume your body, and to say that Aldina Ringwood had told him all about the will. I could purchase his silence only by giving him my daughter, the heiress of The Mere. To this I consented."

As he said these last words, Mr. Maryon sunk heavily into the chair.

The figure of Geoffrey Ringwood placed one ghostly hand upon his left temple, and then passed silently out of the room. I started up, and followed the phantom along the corridor—down the staircase—out at the front door, which still stood open—across the snow-covered lawn—into the plantation; and then it disappeared as strangely as I first had seen it; and, hardly knowing whether I was mad or dreaming, I found my way back to The Shallows.

For some weeks I was ill with brain-fever. When I recovered I was told that terrible things

had happened at The Mere. Mr. Maryon had
been found dead in Sir Henry Benet's room—an
effusion of blood upon the brain, the doctors said
—and the body of Colonel Bludyer had been discovered in the snow· in an old disused gravel-pit
not far from the house.

A year afterward I married Agnes Maryon; and,
if all that I had seen and heard upon that 3d of
February was not merely the invention of a fevered
brain, the debt of honor was at last discharged,
for I, the nephew of the murdered Geoffrey Ringwood, became the owner of The Mere.

DEVEREUX'S DREAM.

DEVEREUX'S DREAM.

I GIVE you this story only at second-hand; but you have it in substance—and he wasted few words over it—as Paul Devereux told it me. It was not the only queer story he could have told about himself if he had chosen, by a good many, I should say. Paul's life had been an eminently unconventional one: the man's face certified to that—hard, bronzed, war-worn, seamed and scarred with strange battle-marks—the face of a man who had dared and done most things.

It was not his custom to speak much of what he had done, however. Probably only because he and I were little likely to meet again that he told me this I am free to tell you now.

We had come across one another for the first time for years that afternoon on the Italian Boulevart. Paul had landed a couple of weeks previously at Marseilles from a long yacht-cruise in southern waters, the monotony of which we heard had been agreeably diversified by a little pirate-hunting and slaver-chasing—the evil tongues called it piracy and slave-running; and certainly Devereux was quite equal to either *métier;* and he was about starting on a promising little filibustering expedition across the Atlantic, where the chances were he would be shot, and the certainty was that he would be starved. So perhaps he felt inclined to be a trifle more communicative than usual, as we sat late that night over a blazing pyre of logs and in a cloud of Cavendish. At all events he was, and after this fashion.

I forget now exactly how the subject was led up to. Expression of some philosophic incredulity on my part regarding certain matters, followed by a ten-minutes' silence on his side pregnant with un-wonted words to come—that was it, perhaps. At last he said, more to himself, it seemed, than to me:

"'Such stuff as dreams are made of.' Well, who knows? You're a Sadducee, Bertie; you call this sort of thing, politely, indigestion. Perhaps you're right. But yet I had a queer dream once."

"Not unlikely," I assented.

"You're wrong; I never dream, as a rule. But, as I say, I had a queer dream once; and queer because it came literally true three years after-ward."

"Queer indeed, Paul."

"Happens to be true. What's queerer still, my dream was the means of my finding a man I owed a long score, and a heavy one, and of my paying him in full."

"Bad for the payee!" I thought.

Paul's face had grown terribly eloquent as he spoke those last words. On a sudden the expres-sion of it changed—another memory was stirring in him. Wonderfully tender the fierce eyes grew; wonderfully tender the faint, sad smile, that was like sunshine on storm-scathed granite. That smile transfigured the man before me.

"Ah, poor child—poor Lucille!" I heard him mutter.

That was it, was it? So I let him be. Presently he lifted his head. If he had let himself get the least thing out of hand for a moment, he had got back his self-mastery the next.

"I'll tell you that queer story, Bertie, if you like," he said.

The proposition was flatteringly unusual, but the voice was quite his own.

"Somehow I'd sooner talk than think about—*her*," he went on after a pause.

I nodded. He might talk about this, you see, but *I* couldn't. He began with a question—an odd one:

"Did you ever hear I'd been married?"

Paul Devereux and a wife had always seemed and been to me a most unheard-of conjunction. So I laconically said:

"No."

"Well, I was once, years ago. She was my wife—that child—for a week. And then——"

I easily filled up the pause; but, as it happened, I filled it up wrongly; for he added:

"And then she was murdered."

I was not unused to our Paul's stony style of talk; but this last sentence was sufficiently startling.

"Eh?"

"Murdered—in her sleep. They never found the man who did it either, though I had Durbec and all the Rue de Jérusalem at work. But I forgave them that, for I found the man myself, and killed him."

He was filling his pipe again as he told me this, and he perhaps rammed the Cavendish in a little tighter, but that was all. The thing was a matter of course; I knew my Paul well enough to know that. Of course he killed him.

"Mind you," he continued, kindling the black *brûle-gueule* the while—"mind you, I'd never seen this man before, never known of his existence, except in a way that—however, it was this way."

He let his grizzled head drop back on the cushions of his chair, and his eyes seemed to see the queer story he was telling enacted once more before him in the red hollows of the fire.

"As I said, it was years ago. I was waiting here in Paris for some fellows who were to join me in a campaign we'd arranged against the African big game. I never was more fit for anything of that sort than I was then. I only tell you this to show you that the thing can't be accounted for by my nerves having been out of order at all.

"Well: I was dining alone that day, at the Café Anglais. It was late when I sat down to my dinner in the little salon as usual. Only two other men were still lingering over theirs. All the time they stayed they bored me so persistently with some confounded story of a murder they were discussing, that I was once or twice more than half-inclined to tell them so. At last, though, they went away.

"But their talk kept buzzing abominably in my head. When the waiter brought me the evening paper, the first thing that caught my eye was a circumstantial account of the *probable* way the fellow did his murder. I say probable, for they never caught him; and, as you will see directly, they could only suppose how it occurred.

"It seemed that a well-known Paris banker, who was ascertained beyond doubt to have left one station alive and well, and with a couple of hundred thousand francs in a leathern *sac* under his seat, arrived at the next station the train stopped at with his throat cut and *minus* all his money, except a few bank-notes to no great amount, which the assassin had been wise enough to leave behind him. The train was a night express on one of the southern lines; the banker travelled quite alone, in a first-class carriage; and the murder must have taken place between midnight and 1 A.M. next morning. The newspapers supposed—rightly enough, I think—that the murderer must have entered the carriage *from without*, stabbed his victim in his sleep—there were no signs of any struggle—opened the *sac*, taken what he wanted, and retreated, loot and all, by the way he came. I fully indorsed my particular writer's opinion that the murderer was an uncommonly cool and clever individual, especially as I fancy he got clear off and was never afterward laid hands on.

"When I had done that I thought I had done with the affair altogether. Not at all. I was regularly ridden with this confounded murder. You see the banker was rather a swell; everybody knew him: and that, of course, made it so shocking. So everybody kept talking about him: they were talking about him at the Opera, and over the *baccarat* and *bouillotte* at La Topaze's later. To escape him I went to bed and smoked myself to sleep. And then a queer thing came to pass: I had a

dream—I who never dream; and this is what I
dreamed:

"I saw a wide, rich country that I knew. A
starless night hung over it like a pall. I saw a
narrow track running through it, straight, both
ways, for leagues. Something sped along this
track with a hurtling rush and roar. This something that at first had looked like a red-eyed devil,
with dark sides full of dim fire, resolved itself, as
I watched it, presently, into a more conventional
night express-train. It flew along, though, as no
express-train ever travelled yet; for all that, I was
able to keep it quite easily in view. I could count
the carriages as they whirled by. One—two—
three—four—five—six; but I could only see distinctly into one. Into that one with perfect distinctness. Into that one I seemed forced to look.

"It was the fourth carriage. Two people were
in it. They sat in opposite corners; both were
sleeping. The one who sat facing forward was a
woman—a girl, rather. I could see that; but I
couldn't see her face. The blind was drawn across
the lamp in the roof, and the light was very dim;
moreover, this girl lay back in the shadow. Yet
I seemed to know her, and I knew that her face was
very fair. She wore a cloak that shrouded her
form completely, yet her form was familiar to me.

"The figure opposite to her was a man's.
Strangely familiar to me too this figure was. But,
as he slept, his head had sunk upon his breast, and
the shadow cast upon his face by the low-drawn
travelling-cap he wore hid it from me. Yet if I had
seemed to know the girl's face, I was certain I knew
the man's. But as I could see, so I could remem-

ber, neither. And there was an absolute torture in this which I can't explain to you,—in this inability, and in my inability to wake them from their sleep.

"From the first I had been conscious of a desire to do that. This desire grew stronger every second. I tried to call to them, and my tongue wouldn't move. I tried to spring toward them, to thrust out my arms and touch them, and my limbs were paralyzed. And then I tried to shut my eyes to what I *knew* must happen, and my eyes were held open and dragged to look on in spite of me. And I saw this:

"I saw the door of the carriage where these two sleepers, whose sleep was so horribly sound, were sitting—I saw this door open, and out of the thick darkness another face look in.

"The light, as I have said, was very dim, but I could see his face as plainly as I can see yours. A large yellow face it was, like a wax mask. The lips were full, and lustful and cruel. The eyes were little eyes of an evil gray. Thin yellow streaks marked the absence of the eyebrows; thin yellow hair showed itself under a huge fur travelling-cap. The whole face seemed to grow slowly into absolute distinctness as I looked, by the sort of devilish light that it, as it were, radiated. I had chanced upon a good many damnable visages before then; but there was a cold fiendishness about this one such as I had seen on no man's face, alive or dead, till then.

"The next moment the man this face belonged to was standing in the carriage, that seemed to plunge and sway more furiously, as though to

5

waken them that still slept on. He wore a long
fur travelling-robe, girt about the waist with a fur
girdle. Abnormally tall and broad as he was, he
looked in this dress gigantic. Yet there was a
marvellous cat-like lightness and agility about all
his movements.

"He bent over the girl lying there helpless in
her sleep. I don't make rash bargains as a rule,
but I felt I would have given years of my life for
five minutes of my lost freedom of limb just then.
I tell you the torture was infernal.

"The assassin—I knew he was an assassin—bent
awhile, gloatingly, over the girl. His great yellow
hands were both bare, and on the forefinger of the
right hand I could see some great stone blazing like
an evil eye. In that right hand there gleamed
something else. I saw him draw it slowly from
his sleeve, and, as he drew it, turn round and
look at the other sleeper with an infernal triumphant malignity and hate the Devil himself
might have envied. But the man he-looked at
slept heavily on. And then—God! I feel the
agony I felt in my dream then now!—then I saw
the great yellow hand, with the great evil eye upon
it, lifted murderously, and the bright steel it held
shimmer as the assassin turned again and bent his
yellow face down closer to that other face hidden
from me in the shadow—the girl's face, that I knew
was so fair.

"How can I tell this? . . . The blade flashed
and fell. . . . There was the sound of a heavy
sigh stifled under a heavy hand. . . .

"Then the huge form of the assassin was reared
erect, and the bloated yellow face seemed to laugh

silently, while the hand that held the steel pointed at the sleeping man in diabolical menace.

"And so the huge form and the bloated yellow face seemed to fade away while I watched.

"The express rushed and roared through the blinding darkness without; the sleeping man slept on still; till suddenly a strong light fell full upon him, and he woke.

"And then I saw why I had been so certain that I knew him. For as he lifted his head, I saw his face in the strong light.

"*And the face was my own face; and the sleeper was myself!*"

Paul Devereux made a pause in his queer story here. Except when he had spoken of the girl, he had spoken in his usual cool, hard way. The pipe he had been smoking all the time was smoked out. He took time to fill another before he went on. I said never a word, for I guessed who the sleeping girl was.

"Well," Paul remarked presently, "that was a devilish queer dream, wasn't it? You'll account for it by telling me I'd been so pestered with the story of the banker's murder that I naturally had nightmare; perhaps, too, that my digestion was out of order. Call it a nightmare, call it dyspepsia, if you like. I *don't*, because—— But you'll see why I don't directly.

"At the same moment that my dream-self awoke in my dream, my actual self woke in reality, and with the same ghastly horror.

"I say the *same* horror, for neither then nor afterward could I separate my one self from my other self. They seemed identical; so that this queer

dream made a more lasting impression upon me
than you'd think. However, in the life I led that
sort of thing couldn't last very long. Before I came
back from Africa I had utterly forgotten all about
it. Before I left Paris, though, and while it was
quite fresh in my memory, I sketched the big murderer just as I had seen him in my dream. The
great yellow face, the great broad frame in the fur
travelling-robe, the great hand with the great evil
eye upon it—everything, carefully and minutely,
as though I had been going to paint a portrait that
I wanted to make lifelike. I think at the time I
had some such intention. If I had, I never fulfilled
it. But I made the sketch, as I say, carefully;
and then I forgot all about it.

"Time passed—three years nearly. I was win-
tering in the south of France that year. There it
was that I met her—Lucille. Old D'Avray, her
father, and I had met before in Algeria. He was
dying now. He left the child on his death-bed to
me. The end was I married her.

"Poor little thing! I think I might have made
her happy—who knows? She used to tell me often
she was happy with me. Poor little thing!

"Well, we were to come straight to London.
That was Lucille's notion. She wanted to go to
my London first—nowhere else. Now I would
rather have gone anywhere else; but, naturally, I
let the child have her way. She seemed nervously
eager about it, I remembered afterward; seemed
to have a nervous objection to every other place I
proposed. But I saw or suspected nothing to make
me question her very closely, or the reasons for her
preference for our grimy old Pandemonium. What

could I suspect? Not the truth. If I only had!
If I had only guessed what it was that made her,
as she said, long to be safe there already. Safe?
What had she to fear with me? Ah, what indeed!

"So we started on our journey to England. It
was a cold, dark night, early in March. We
reached Lyons somewhere about seven. I should
have stayed there that night but for Lucille. She
entreated me so earnestly and with such strange
vehemence to go on by the night-mail to Paris, that
at last, to satisfy her, I consented; though it struck
me unpleasantly at the time that I had let her travel
too long already, and that this feverishness was the
consequence of over-fatigue. But she became paci-
fied at once when I told her it should be as she
wanted; and declared she should sleep perfectly
well in the carriage with me beside her. She
should feel quite safe then, she said.

"Safe! Where safer? you might ask. Nowhere, I believe. Alone with me—surely nowhere
safer. The Paris express was a short train that
night; but I managed to secure a compartment for
ourselves. I left Lucille in her corner there while
I went across to the *buffet* to fill a flask. I was
gone barely five minutes; but when I came back
the change in the child's face fairly startled me.
I had seen it last with the smile it always wore for-
me on it, looking so childishly happy in the lamp-
light. Now it was all gray-pale and distorted; and
the great blue eyes told me directly with what.

"Fear—sudden, terrible fear—I thought. But
fear? Fear of what? I asked her. She clung
close to me half-sobbing awhile before she could
answer; and then she told me—nothing. There

was nothing the matter; only she had felt a pain—
a cruel pain—at her heart; and it had frightened
her. Yes, that was it; it had frightened her, but
it had passed; and she was well, quite well again
now.

"All this time her eyes seeemd to be telling me
another story; but I said nothing; she was obviously too excited already. I did my best to soothe her,
and I succeeded. She told me she felt quite well
once more before we started. No, she had rather,
much rather go on to Paris, as I had promised her
she should. She should sleep all the way, if no one
came into the carriage to disturb her. No one could
come in? Then nothing could be better.

"And so it was that she and I started that night
by the Paris mail.

"I made her up a bed of rugs and wraps upon
the cushions; but she had rather rest her head upon
my shoulder, she said, and feel my arm about her;
nothing could hurt her then. Ah, strange how she
harped on that.

"She lay there, then, as she loved best—with
her head resting on my shoulder, not sleeping much
or soundly; uneasily, with sudden waking starts,
and with glances round her; till I would speak to
her. And then she would look up into my face and
smile; and so drop into that uneasy sleep again.
And I would think she was over-tired, that was
all; and reproach myself with having let her come
on. And three or four hours passed like this; and
then we had got as far as Dijon.

"But the child was fairly worn out now; and she
offered no opposition when I asked her to let me
pillow her head on something softer than my

shoulder. So I folded a great thick shawl she was too well cloaked to need, and she made that her pillow.

"We were rushing full swing through the wild, dark night, when she lifted up her face and bade me kiss her and bid her sleep well. And I put my arm round her, and kissed the child's loving lips —for the last time while she lived. Then I flung myself on the seat opposite her; and, watching her till she slept soundly and peacefully, slept at last myself also. I had drawn the blind across the lamp in the roof, and the light in the carriage was very dim.

"How long I slept I don't know; it couldn't have been more than an hour and a half, because the express was slackening speed for its first halt beyond Dijon. I had slept heavily I knew; but I woke with a sudden, sharp sense of danger that made me broad awake, and strung every nerve in a moment. The sort of feeling you have when you wake on a prairie, where you have come across 'Indian sign;' on outpost-duty, when your *feld-webel* plucks gently at your cloak. You know what I mean.

"I was on my feet at once. As I said, the light in the carriage was very dim, and the shadow was deepest where Lucille lay. I looked there instinctively. She must have moved in her sleep, for her face was turned away from me; and the cloak I had put so carefully about her had partly fallen off. But she slept on still. Only soundly, very soundly; she scarcely seemed to breathe. And—*did* she breathe?

"A ghastly fear ran through my blood, and froze

it. I understood why I had wakened. In my nostrils was an awful odor that I knew well enough. I bent over her; I touched her. Her face was very cold; her eyes glared glassily at me; my hands were wet with something. My hands were wet with blood—her blood!

"I tore away the blind from the lamp, and then I could see that my wife of a week lay there stabbed straight to the heart—dead—dead beyond doubting; murdered in her sleep."

Devereux's stern, low voice shook ever so little as he spoke those last words; and we both sat very silent after them for a good while. Only when he could trust his utterance again he went on.

"A curious piece of devilry, wasn't it? That child—whom had she ever harmed? Who could hate her like this? I remember I thought that, in a dull, confused sort of way, when I found myself alone in that carriage with her lying dead on the cushions before me. *Alone* with her—you understand? It was confusing.

"I pass over what immediately followed. The express came duly to a halt; and then I called people to me, and—and the Paris express went on without that particular carriage.

"The inquiry began before some local authority next day. Very little came of it. What could come of it, unless they had convicted *me* of the murder of this child I would have given my own life to save?

"They might have done that at home; but they knew better here, and didn't. They couldn't find me the actual assassin, however; though I believe they did their best. All they found was his weapon,

which he must purposely have left behind. I asked
for this, and got it. It gave their police no clue;
and it gave me none. But I had a fancy for it.

"It was a plain, double-edged, admirably-tem-
pered dagger—a very workmanlike article indeed.
On the cross hilt of it I swore one day that I would
live thenceforth for one thing alone—the discovery
of the murderer of old D'Avray's child, whom I had
promised him to care for before all. When I had
found this man, whoever he was, I also swore that
I would kill him. Kill him myself, you understand; without any of the law's delay or uncer-
tainty, without troubling *bourreau* or hangman.
Kill him as he had killed her—to do this was what
I meant to live for. There was war to the knife
between him and me.

"I started, of course, under one heavy disadvan-
tage. He knew me, probably, whereas I didn't
know him at all. When he found that his amiable
intention of fixing the crime on me had been frustrated, it must,·I imagined, have occurred to him
that the said crime might eventually be fixed by me
on him. And he had proved himself to be a person
who didn't stick at trifles. It behooved me, therefore, to go to work cautiously. But I hadn't fought
Indians for nothing; and I *was* very cautious. I
waited quiet till I got a clue. It was a curious
one; and I got it in this way. It struck me one
day, suddenly, that I had heard of a murder precisely similar to this already. I could not at first
call the thing to mind; but presently I remembered—my dream. And then I asked myself this:
*Had not this murder been done before my eyes three
years ago?*

"I came to the conclusion that the circumstances of the murder in my dream were absolutely identical with the circumstances of the actual crime. Yes; the girl whose face in that dream I had never been able to see was Lucille. ¹ Yes; the assassin whose face I had seen so plainly in that dream was the real assassin. In short, I believe that the murder had been *rehearsed* before me three years previous to its actual committal.

"Now this sounds rather wild. Yet I came to this conviction quite coolly and deliberately. It *was* a conviction. Assuming it to be true, the odds against me grew shorter directly; *for I had the portrait of the man I wanted drawn by myself the day after I had seen him in my dream.* And the original of that portrait was a man not to be easily mistaken, supposing him to exist at all. The day I came across that sketch of him in that old forgotten sketch-book of mine, I was as sure he did exist as that I was alive myself. What I had to do was to find this man, and then I never doubted I should find the man I wanted. You see how the odds had shortened. If he knew me I knew him now, and he had no notion that I did know him. It was a good deal fairer fight between us.

"I fought it out alone. My story was hardly one the Rue de Jérusalem would have acted upon; and, besides, I wanted no interference. So, with the portrait before me, I sat down and began to consider who this man was, and why he had murdered that child. The big, burly frame, the heavy yellow face, the sandy-yellow hair, the physiognomy generally, was Teutonic. My man I put down as a North German. Now there were, and are probably, plenty of men who would have no objection whatever to put a knife into me, if they got the chance; but this man, whom I had never met, could have had no such quarrel as theirs with me. His quarrel with me must have been, then, Lucille. Yes, that was it—Lucille. I began to see clearly: a thwarted, devilish passion—a cool, infernal revenge. The child had feared something of this sort; had perhaps seen him that night. This explained her nervous terror, her nervous anxiety to stop nowhere, to travel on. In that carriage of that express-train, alone with me—where could she be safer? This accounted, too, for her anxiety to reach England. He would not dare follow her there, she had thought, or, at least, could not without my noticing him. And then she would have told me. She had not told me before evidently because she had feared for *me* too, in a quarrel with this man. She must, innocent child as she was, have had some instinctive knowledge of what he was capable. . . . Ay, a cool, infernal revenge, indeed. To kill her; to fix the murder on me. That dagger he had left behind. . . . The apparent impossibility of any one's entering the carriage as he must have entered it at all, to say nothing of the almost absolute impossibility of his doing so without disturbing either of us,—you see it might have gone hard with me if a British jury had had to decide on the case.

"Well, to cut this as short as may be, I made up my mind that the man I wanted was a North German; that he had conceived a hideous passion for Lucille before I knew her; that she had shrunk from it and him so unmistakably, that he knew he

had no chance; that my taking her away as my
wife, to which he might have been a witness, drove
him to as hideous a revenge; that, hearing we were
going to England, and seeing that we were likely
to stop nowhere on the way, and so give him a
chance of doing what he had made up his mind to
do, he had decided to do what he had done as he
had done it,—counting on finding us asleep as he
had found us, or on his strength if it came to a fight
between him and me; but coolly reckless enough to
brave everything in any case. And the devil aiding, he had in great part and only too well succeeded. He was now either so far satisfied that, if
I made no move against him—and how, he might
think, could I?—he, feeling himself all safe, would
let me be; or, on the other hand, he did not feel
safe, and was not satisfied, and was arranging for
my being disposed of by and by. I considered the
latter frame of mind as his most probable one; I
went to work cautiously, as I say. I ascertained
that Lucille had made no mention of any obnoxious
prétendant at any time; I didn't expect to find she
had, her terror of the man was too intense. But
this man must have met her somewhere—where?

"When old D'Avray came home to die, his
daughter was just leaving her Paris *pensionnat*.
All through his last illness he had seen no visitor
but me, and Lucille had never quitted him. Besides, I had been there all the time. I presumed,
then, that this man and she had met in Paris; and
I believe they were only likely to have met at one
of the half-dozen houses where the child would now
and again be asked. I got a list of all these. One
name only struck me; it happened to be a German

name—Steinmetz. I wondered if Monsieur Steinmetz was my man. In the mean time, who was he?
I had no trouble in finding that out: Monsieur
Steinmetz was a German banker of good standing
and repute, reasonably well off, and recently left
a widower. Personally? *Dame*, personally Monsieur Steinmetz was a great man and a fat, with a
big face and blond hair, and the appearance of what
he really was—a *bon vivant* and a *bon enfant* yet
n'avait jamais fait de mal à personne—allez !—
All, yes; in effect, Madame had died about a year
ago, and Monsieur had been inconsolable for a long
time. He had changed his residence now, and inhabited a house in one of the new streets off the
Champs Elysées.

"From another source I discovered that in the
lifetime of Madame Steinmetz Lucille was frequently at the house. She had ceased to come there
about the date of the commencement of Madame's
sudden illness. I got this information by degrees,
while I lay *perdu* in an old haunt of mine in the
Pays Latin yonder; for I had always had an idea
that I should find the man I wanted in Paris. When
I had got it, I thought I should like to see Monsieur Steinmetz, the agreeable banker. One night I
strolled up as far as his new residence in the street
off the Champs Elysées. Monsieur Steinmetz lived
on the first-floor. There was a brilliant light there:
Monsieur Steinmetz was entertaining friends, it
seemed.

"It was a fine night; I established myself out
of sight under the doorway of an unfinished house
opposite, and waited. I don't know why; perhaps
I fancied that when his friends were gone, the fine-

ness of the night might induce Monsieur Steinmetz
to take a stroll, and that then I should be able to
gratify my curiosity. You see, I knew that if he
were my man, I should know him directly. I
waited a good while: shadows crossed the lighted
blinds; once a big, broad shadow appeared there,
that made me fancy I mightn't have been waiting for
nothing after all, somehow. Presently Monsieur
Steinmetz's guests departed, and in a little while
after there appeared on the little balcony of Monsieur Steinmetz's apartment *the man I wanted.*
There was a moon that night, and the cold white
light fell on the great yellow face, with the full
lustful lips, and the full cruel chin, just as I had
seen the light fall on it in my dream. It was the
same face, Bertie; the same face, the same man.
I couldn't be mistaken. I had no doubt; I *knew*
that the assassin of my wife, of that tender, innocent, helpless child, stood there, twenty yards from
me, on that balcony.

"I had got myself pretty well in hand; and it
was as well. I never moved. The face I knew
turned presently toward the spot where I stood
hidden,—the face I had seen in my dream, beyond
all doubting. The evil gray eyes glanced careless-
ly into the shadow, and up and down the quiet
street; and then Monsieur Steinmetz, humming an
air, got inside the window again, and closed it after
him. Once more the great burly shadow that had
at first told me I should not wait in that dark doorway in vain crossed the blinds; and then it disappeared. I saw my man no more that night; but I
had seen enough. I knew who he was now, and
where to find him.

" As I walked along home I thought what I would do. I quite meant to kill Monsieur Steinmetz; but I also meant to have no *démêlés* with an Impérial Procureur and the Cour d'Assizes for doing so. I didn't want to murder him, either. I thought I would wait a little for the chance of a suitable opportunity for settling my business satisfactorily. And I did wait. I turned this delay to account, and got together a case of circumstantial evidence against my man that, though perhaps it might have broken down in a law-court, would have been alone amply sufficient for me.

" The reason why Lucille's visits to the banker's house ceased was, it appeared, because Madame Steinmetz had conceived all at once a jealous dislike to her. How far this was owing to Lucille herself I could well understand; but I could understand Madame's jealousy equally well. Madame's illness, strangely sudden, dated from the cessation of Lucille's visits. Was it hard to find a *cause* for that illness—a cause for the wife's subsequent suspected death? I thought not. Then had followed Lucille's departure from Paris. The child's anxiety for her father hid her *other fear* from his eyes and mine; but that fear must have been on her then. With us she forgot it in time; yet it or another reason had always prevented all mention of what had occasioned it. She became my wife. At that very time I easily ascertained that Steinmetz was absent from Paris; less easily, but indubitably, that he had, at all events, been as far south as Lyons. At Lyons it must have been that Lucille first discovered he was dogging us. Hence her alarm, which I had remembered, and her anxiety to proceed on our journey without stopping for the night, as I had previously arranged. The morning after the murder Steinmetz reappeared in Paris. From the hour at which he was seen at the *gare*, it was certain that he had travelled by the night express train in which Lucille and I had started from Lyons; and he wore that morning a travelling-coat of fur in all respects similar to the one I remembered so well.

"If I had ever had any doubt of my man after actually seeing him, I should probably have convinced myself that he was my man by the general tendency of these facts, which I got at slowly and one by one. But I had no need of such evidence; and of course no case, even with such evidence, for a court of law. However, courts of law I had never intended to trouble in the matter.

"The opportunity I was waiting was some time before it offered. Monsieur Steinmetz was a man of regular habits, I found—from his first-floor in the street off the Champs Elysées, every morning at eleven, to the Bourse; thence to his bureau hard by till four; from his bureau to his café, where he read papers and played dominoes till six; and then home slowly by the Boulevarts. He might consider himself tolerably safe from me while he led this sort of life, even supposing he was aware he was incurring any danger. I don't think he troubled much about that; till one night, when, over the count of the beloved domino-points, his eyes met mine fixed right upon him. I had arranged this little surprise to see how it would affect him.

"Perhaps my gaze may have expressed something more than the mere distraction I intended; but I

noticed—though a more indifferent observer might
easily have failed to notice—how the great yellow
face, expanded in childish interest in the childish
game, seemed suddenly to grow gray and harden;
how the fat smile became a cruel baring of sharp
white teeth; how the fat chin squared itself. The
man knew me, and scented danger.

"A moment's reflection convinced Monsieur
Steinmetz, though, that it could be by no means so
certain that I knew him; five minutes' observation
of me more than half satisfied him that I did not.
Yet what did I want there? What was I doing in
Paris? This might concern him nearly, he must
have thought.

"I kept my own face in order, and watched his.
It wasn't an easy one to read; but you see I had
studied it closely, and in a way he couldn't have
dreamed of. Monsieur Steinmetz was outwardly
his wonted self, but inwardly not quite comfortable
when he rose; and I saw the evil eye gleam on his
great yellow finger as he took out his purse to pay
the *garçon*, just as I had seen it when that finger
pointed at *myself* in my dream. I felt curious sensations, Bertie, as I sat there and looked abstractedly at Monsieur Steinmetz. I wondered how long it
would be before—— But my time hadn't come yet.
He went out without another glance at me. I saw
his huge form on the other side of the street when
I left the café in my turn. This I had expected.
Monsieur Steinmetz was naturally curious. It was
hardly possible that I could know him; but it was
quite certain that he ought to know all about me.
So, when I moved on, he moved on; in short, Monsieur Steinmetz dogged me up one street and down

6

another, till he finally dogged me home to my hiding-place in the Pays Latin. He did it very well, too—much better than you would have expected from so apparently unwieldy a *mouchard*. But I *remembered* how lightly he could move.

"Next day I had, of course, disappeared from my old quarters, and gone no one knew where. I suppose Monsieur Steinmetz didn't like this fact when he heard of it. It might have seemed suspicious. Suppose I *had* recognized him? In that case I had evidently a little game of my own, and was as evidently desirous to keep it dark. He was a cool hand; but I fancy my man began to get a little uneasy. He took some trouble to find me again. After a while I permitted him to do that. Once found, he seemed determined that I should not be lost sight of again for want of watching. I permitted that, too; it helped play my game, and I wanted to bring it to an end. To which intent, Monsieur Steinmetz got to hear from sources best known to himself as much of my plans as should bring him to the state I wanted. That was a murderous state. I wanted to get him to think that I was dangerous enough to be worth putting out of the way. I presume he was aware there were, or would be, weak joints in his armor, impenetrable as it seemed; and he preferred not risking the ordeal of legal battle if he could help it. At all events, he elected at last to rid himself of a person who might be dangerous, and was troublesome, by the shortest and the simplest means.

"I say so because when, believing my man was ripe for this, I left Paris about midday for a certain secluded little spot on the sea-coast, I saw one of

Monsieur Steinmetz's employees on the platform;
and because, two days after my arrival in my secluded spot, I met Monsieur Steinmetz in person,.
newly arrived also. Now this was exactly what I
had intended and anticipated. Monsieur Steinmetz
had come down there to put me out of his way, if
he could. He passed me, leisurely strolling in the
opposite direction, humming his favorite *aria*, big-
ger and yellower than ever, the evil eye fiery on his
finger. His own eyes shot me as evil fire; but he
said nothing. . . . I saw he was ripe, though. . . .
My time was close at hand.

"It came. Monsieur Steinmetz and I met once
more in the very place where I, knowing my
ground, had intended we should meet. It was a
dip in the cliffs like a hollowed palm, and just
there the cliff jutted out a good bit, with a sheer fall
on to the rocks below. It was a gray afternoon, at
the end of summer. The wind was rising fast;
there was a thunder of heavy waves already.

"I think he had been dogging me; but I hadn't
chosen to let him get up to me till now. We were
quite out of sight when he had reached the level
bottom of the dip, where I had halted—quite out
of sight, and quite alone. To do him justice, he
came on steadily enough. His face was liker the
sketch I had made of it, liker the face I had seen in
my dream, than it had ever looked before. Evidently he had made up his mind. . . . At last,
then! . . . Well, I had been waiting long! . . .
He was close beside me.

"'*Ah! bon jour, cher Monsieur Steinmetz.*'

"'So?' he said, his little eyes contracting like a
cobra's. 'Ah! Monsieur knows my name?'

"'Among other things about you—yes.'

"'So!' The yellow face was turning grayer and harder every minute—liker and liker to my likeness of it. "And what other things? Has it never appeared to you that this you do, have been doing—this meddling, may be dangerous, *hein?*'

"He had changed his tone, as he had changed the person in which he addressed me. Yes, he had certainly made up his mind. And his big right hand was hidden inside his waistcoat, so that I could not see the evil eye I knew was on his finger.

"'Dangerous?' he repeated slowly.

"'Possibly.'

"'Ay, surely; I shall crush you!'

"'Try.'

"'In good time; wait. You plot against me. Take care; I am strong; I warn you. There must be an end of this, you understand, or——'

"He nodded his big head significantly.

"'You are right,' I told him; 'there must be an end. It is coming.'

"'So?'

"'Yes; I know you. You know me now.'

"'I know you. What do you want?'

"'To kill you.'

"'So?'

"'Yes; as you killed her.'

"'As I killed her? That is it, then? You know that?'

"'I know that.'

"'Well, it is true. I killed her. Now you can guess what I am going to do to you—to you, curse you!—whom she loved.'

"THE GREAT YELLOW FACE LOOKED SILENTLY UP AT ME; AND THEN
—THEN IT DISAPPEARED."

"The very face I had seen in my dream now, Bertie, the very face! There was something besides the evil eye that gleamed in his right hand when he drew it from his breast. Once more he spoke.

"'Yes, I killed her. I meant worse for you. You escaped that; but you will not escape me now. Fool! were you mad to do this? Did not I hate you enough? And I would have let you be. Ah, die, then, if you will have it so!'

"His heavy right arm swung high as he spoke, and I saw the sharp steel gleam as it turned to fall. And I twisted from his grip, and caught the falling arm, and bent it till the dagger dropped to the ground. And then, for a fierce, desperate, devilish minute, I had him in my clutch, dragging him nearer the smooth, slippery edge. He was no match for me at this I knew, and he knew; but he held me with the hold of his despair, and I could not loose myself. Both of us together, he meant; but not I. Yet I only freed myself just as he rolled exhausted, but clutching at the tough, short bushes wildly, toward the brink, and partly over it. . . . Only the hold of his hands between him and his death. And I knelt above him, with the knife in my hand that was stained with *her* blood.

"The great yellow face, ashen now in its mortal agony, looked silently up at me—for three or four awful seconds; and then—then it disappeared.

"Bah!" Paul concluded, "that was the end of it."

CATHERINE'S QUEST.

CATHERINE'S QUEST.

IMAGINE to yourself an old, rambling, red-brick house, with odd corners and gables here and there, all bound and clasped together with ivy, and you have Craymoor Grange. It was built long before Queen Elizabeth's time, and that illustrious monarch is said to have slept in it in one of her royal progresses—as where has she not slept?

There still remain some remnants of bygone ages, although it has been much modernized and added to in later days. Among these are the brewhouse and laundry—formerly, it is said, dining-hall and ball-room. The latter of these is chiefly remarkable for an immense arched window, such as you see in churches, with five lights.

When we came to the Grange this window had been partially blocked up, and in front of it, up to one-third of its height, was a wooden daïs, or platform, on which stood a cumbrous mangle, left there, I suppose, by the last tenants of the house.

Of these last tenants we knew very little, for it was so long since it had been inhabited that the oldest authority in the village could not remember it.

There were, however, some half-defaced monuments in the village church of Craymoor, bearing the figures and escutcheons of knights and dames of "the old family," as the villagers said; but the

inscriptions were worn and almost illegible, and
for some time we none of us took the pains to decipher them.

We first came to Craymoor Grange in the summer of 1849, my husband having discovered the
place in one of his rambles, and taken a fancy to
it. At first I certainly thought we could never
make it our home, it was so dilapidated and tum-
ble-down; but by the time winter came on we had
had several repairs done and alterations made, and
the rooms really became quite presentable.

As our family was small we confined ourselves
chiefly to the newest part of the house, leaving the
older rooms to the mice, dust, and darkness. We
made use of two of the old rooms, however, one as
a servants' bedroom and the other as an extra
spare chamber, in case of many visitors. For myself, though I hope I am neither nervous nor
superstitious, I confess that I would rather sleep
in "our wing," as we called the part of the house
we inhabited, than in any of the old rooms.

When Catherine l'Estrange came to us, however, during our first Christmas at Craymoor, I
found that she was troubled with no such fancies,
but declared that she delighted in queer old rooms,
with raftered ceilings and deep window-seats, such
as ours, and begged to be allowed to occupy the
spare chamber. This I readily acceded to, as we
had several visitors, and needed all the available
rooms.

As my story has principally to do with Catherine l'Estrange, I suppose I ought to speak more
fully about her. She was an old school-friend of
my daughter Ella, and at the time of which I am

speaking was just one-and-twenty, and the merriest girl I ever knew. She had stayed with us once or twice before we came to the Grange, but we then knew no other particulars concerning her family, than that her father had been an Indian officer, and that he and her mother had both died in India when she was about six years old, leaving her to the care of an aunt living in England.

I now, after a long, and I fear a tedious, preamble, come to my story.

On the eve of the new year of 1850, Catherine had a very bad sore throat, and was obliged, though sorely against her inclination, to stay in bed all day, and forego our small evening gayety.

At about 6 o'clock P.M., Ella took her some tea, and fearing she would be dull, offered to stay with her during the evening. This, however, · Catherine would not hear of. "You go and entertain your company," said she laughingly, "and leave me to my own devices; I feel very lazy, and I dare say I shall go to sleep." As she had not slept much on the preceding night, Ella thought it was the best thing she could do; so she went out by the door leading on to the corridor, first placing the night-lamp on a table behind the door opening on to the laundry, so that it might not shine in her face.

She did not again visit Catherine's room until reminded to do so by my son George, at about half-past ten. She then rapped at the door, and receiving no answer, opened it softly, and approached the bed. Catherine lay quite still, and Ella imagined her to be asleep. She therefore returned to the drawing-room without disturbing her,

As it was New Year's eve, we stayed up "to see the old year out and the new year in," and at a few minutes to twelve we all gathered round the open window on the stairs to hear the chimes ring out from the village church.

We were all listening breathlessly as the hall-clock struck twelve, when a piercing cry suddenly echoed through the house, causing us all to start in alarm. I knew that it could only proceed from Catherine's room, for the servants were all assembled at the window beneath us, listening, like ourselves, for the chimes. Thither therefore I flew, followed by Ella, and we found poor Catherine in a truly pitiable state.

She was deadly pale, in an agony of terror, and the perspiration stood in large drops upon her forehead. It was some time before we could succeed at all in composing her, and her first words were to implore us to take her into another room.

She was too weak to stand, so we wrapped her in blankets, and carried her into Ella's bedroom. I noticed that as she was taken through the laundry she shuddered, and put her hands before her eyes. When she was laid on Ella's bed she grew calmer, and apologized for the trouble she had caused, saying that she had had a dreadful dream.

With this explanation we were fain to be content, though I thought it hardly accounted for her excessive terror. I had observed, however, that any allusion to what had passed caused her to tremble and turn pale again, and I thought it best to refrain from exciting her further.

When morning came I found Catherine almost

her usual self again; but I persuaded her to remain in bed until the evening, as her cold was not much better. Ella's curiosity to hear the dream which had so much excited her friend could now no longer be restrained; but whenever she asked to hear it, Catherine said, "Not now; another time, perhaps, I may tell you."

When she came down to dinner in the evening; we noticed that she was peculiarly silent, and we endeavored to rally her into her usual spirits, but in vain. She tried to laugh and to appear merry, poor child; but there was evidently something on her mind.

At last, as we all sat round the fire after dinner, she spoke. She addressed herself to my husband, but the tone of her voice caused us all to listen.

"Mr. Fanshawe, I have something to ask of you," said she, and then paused.

"Ask on," said Mr. Fanshawe.

"I know that you will think the request I am going to make a peculiar one; but I have a particular reason for making it," continued she. "It is that you will have the wooden daïs in front of the laundry window removed."

Mr. Fanshawe certainly was taken aback, as were we all. When he had mastered his bewilderment, and assured himself that he had heard aright—

"It is, indeed, a strange request, my dear Catherine," said he; "what can be your reason for asking such a thing?"

"If you will only have it done, and not question me, you will understand my reason," answered Catherine.

Mr. Fanshawe demurred, however, thinking it some foolish whim, and at last Catherine said:

"I must tell you why I wish it done, then: I am sure we shall discover something underneath."

At this we all looked at one another in extreme bewilderment.

"Discover something underneath? No doubt ·we should—cobwebs, probably, and dust and spiders," answered Mr. Fanshawe, much amused.

But Catherine was not to be laughed down.

"Only do as I wish," said she beseechingly, "and you will see. If you find nothing underneath the daïs but cobwebs and dust, then you may laugh at me as much as you like." And I saw that she was serious, for tears were actually gathering in her eyes. Of course we were all very anxious to know what Catherine expected to find, and how she came to suspect that there was anything to be found; but she would not say, and begged us all not to question her.

And now George took upon himself to interfere.

"Let us do as Catherine wishes, father," said he; "the daïs spoils the laundry, and would be much better away."

"Well, well," said Mr. Fanshawe, "do as you like, only I shall expect my share of the treasure that is found.—And now," added he, "you must have a glass of wine to warm you, Catherine, for you look sadly pale, child."

Here the conversation changed, though we often alluded to the subject again during the evening.

The next morning the first thing in all our thoughts was Catherine's singular request.

I think Mr. Fanshawe had hoped she would

have forgotten it, but such was not the case; on the contrary, she enlisted George's services the first thing after breakfast to carry out her design, and they left the room together, accompanied by Ella.

It was a snowy morning, and Mr. Fanshawe was obliged to be away from home all day on business, so I was quite at a loss how to entertain my numerous guests successfully. Happily for me, however, the mystery attendant on the removal of the daïs in the laundry charmed them all; and I have to thank Catherine for contributing to their amusement much better than I could possibly have done.

Not long after the disappearance of Catherine, Ella, and George, a message was sent to us in the drawing-room requesting our presence in the laundry; and on all flocking there with more or less eagerness, we found a fire burning on the old-fashioned hearth and chairs arranged round it.

It appeared that with the help of Sam, our factotum, who was a kind of Jack-of-all-trades, George had succeeded in loosening the planks of the daïs, which, although strongly put together, were rotten and worm-eaten, and that we were now summoned to be witnesses of its removal. We found Catherine trembling with a strange eagerness, and her face quite pale with excitement. This was shared by Ella and George; and, judging by the important expression on their faces, I fancied they were let further into the secret than any one else.

We all sat down in the chairs placed for our accommodation, and the wild whistling of the wind in the huge chimney, "together with the sheets of snow which darkened the window-panes, enhanced the mystery of the whole affair, while George and his coadjutor worked lustily on.

At length, after a great deal of panting and puffing, George was heard to exclaim, "Now for the tug of war!" and there followed a minute's pause, and then a crash as the loosened planks were torn asunder, and a cloud of dust enveloped both workmen and spectators.

Involuntarily we all started forward, and a moment of the direst confusion ensued, during which the boys of our party greatly endangered their limbs among the broken boards.

"By George!" exclaimed my son at last—in his eagerness invoking his patron saint—as he stumbled upon something, "there is something here and no mistake;" and, hastily clearing away the rubbish and clinging cobwebs, he disclosed to view what proved on examination to be an immense oaken chest, about four feet in height, heavily carved, and ornamented with brass mouldings corroded with age and damp.

Here was a piece of excitement indeed; never in my most imaginative moments had I thought of anything so mysterious as this. The most sceptical among us grew interested.

"Oh, do open it!" cried Ella, when the first exclamations of surprise were over.

"Easier to say than to do, miss," replied Sam, exerting his Herculean strength in vain. With the aid of a hammer and the kitchen-poker, however, he at last succeeded in forcing it open. We all pressed forward eagerly to peer inside. There was something in it certainly, but we none of us

could determine what, until Sam, who was the
boldest of us all, thrust in his hand and brought
forth—something which caused the bravest to start
with horror, while poor Catherine sank down,
white and trembling, upon the littered floor. It
was a bone, to which adhered fragments of decay-
ing silk.

The consternation and conjectures which followed can be better imagined than described.
Seeing the effects of the discovery upon Catherine,
and indeed upon all, I bade Sam replace it in the
chest, which George closed again, to be left until
Mr. Fanshawe came home and could investigate
the matter.

The rest of the day I passed in attending to
Catherine, who seemed much shocked and overcome by what she had seen, and in trying to divert my guests' thoughts from the subject, and
dispel the gloom which had gathered over all. In
this I succeeded only partially, and never did I
welcome my husband's return more gladly than on
that evening.

On his arrival I would not let him be disturbed
by the relation of what had happened until he had
finished his dinner, and it was not till we were
gathered as usual round the fire that George related
the whole story to him.

When he ended the two gentlemen left the room
together, in order that Mr. Fanshawe might verify
by his own eyes what he would hardly believe.

They were some time gone, and on their return
I noticed that my husband held in his hand an old
piece of soiled parchment, with mouldy seals
affixed to it.

7

"We certainly have discovered much more than I thought for, Catherine," said he, "and possibly more than you thought for either." Here he paused for her to reply, but she did not.

"The bones are most probably those of some animal," added he—I fancied I could detect a certain anxiety in his tone that belied what he said; "but in order to quell the active imaginations which I can see are running away with some of you"—here he looked round with a smile—"I will send for Dr. Driscoll to come and examine them to-morrow. I have also found a piece of parchment in the chest," he added; "but I have not yet looked at its contents."

"Before you do that, Mr. Fanshawe, and before you send for the surgeon," interrupted Catherine suddenly in a clear voice, "I think I can tell you all about the bones found in the chest, and how I guessed them to be there."

"I should certainly be very glad to be told," my husband admitted, much surprised; "though how you can possibly know, I cannot surmise."

"Listen, and I will tell you," answered Catherine; and feeling very glad that our curiosity was at last to be gratified, we all "pricked up our ears," as George would say, to listen.

I here transcribe Catherine's story word for word, as my son George subsequently wrote it down from her dictation.

"You all remember," she began, "my alarming you on New Year's eve at midnight, and that I told you I was disturbed by a dreadful dream.

"I said so because I thought you would make

fun of me if I called it a vision; and yet it was much more like a vision, for I seemed to see it waking, and it was more vivid and consecutive than any dream I ever had.

"Before I try to describe it, I want you all to understand that I seemed intuitively to comprehend what I saw, and to recognize all the figures which appeared before me, and their relation to one another, though I am sure I never beheld them before in my life.

"When Ella left me that night, I lay propped up with pillows, staring idly at the strange shadows thrown by the hidden lamp across the laundry ceiling and over the floor. As I looked it seemed to me that a change came over the room— a most unaccountable change.

"Instead of the blocked-up window, the rusty mangle, and the daïs at the farther end, I saw the window clear and distinct from top to bottom, and in front of a deep window-seat at its base stood an oaken chest, exactly corresponding to the one discovered this morning. The room seemed brilliantly lighted, and everything was clearly and distinctly visible; and not only was it changed, but also peopled.

"Many figures passed up and down; brocaded silks swept the floor, and old-world forms of men in strange costumes bowed in courtly style to the dames by their side. Among all these figures I noticed only one couple particularly, and I knew them to be bride and bridegroom. The man was tall and broad, with dark hair and eyes, and a sensual and cruel face. He seemed, however, to be quite enslaved by the woman by his side, whom

I hardly even now like to think of, there was something to me so repellent in her presence.

"She was tall and of middle age, and would have been handsome were it not for a sinister expression in her dark flashing eyes, which was enhanced by the black eyebrows which met over them.

"She reminded me irresistibly of the effigy on the stone monument in Craymoor church, which Ella and I named "the wicked woman."

"As I gazed on the strange scene before me I presently became aware of three other figures which I had not noticed before. They were standing in a small arched doorway in one corner of the room (where the servants' bedroom now is) furtively watching the gay company. One was a pale, careworn woman, apparently of about five-and-thirty, still beautiful, though haggard and mournful-looking, with blue eyes and a fair complexion.

"Her hands rested on the shoulders of two children, one a boy and the other a girl, of about ten and eleven years of age respectively. They much resembled their mother, and, like her, they were meanly dressed, though no poverty of attire could hide the nobility of their aspect. I noticed that the mother's eyes rested chiefly on the face of the tall stately man' before mentioned, who seemed unaware or careless of her presence; and instinctively I knew him to be the father of her children and the blighter of her life.

"As I looked and beheld all this, the lights vanished, the company disappeared, and the room became dark and deserted. No, not quite deserted, for I presently distinguished, seated on the window-seat by the old oaken chest, the fair woman and her children again.

"The moonlight now streamed through the window upon the woman's face, making it appear more ghastly and haggard than before. In her long thin fingers she was holding up to the light a necklace of large pearls, curiously interwoven in a diamond pattern, and on this the children's eyes were fixed.

"She then hung it on the girl's fair neck, who hid it in her bosom. Both children then twined their arms round their mother and kissed her repeatedly, while her head sank lower and lower, and the paleness of death overspread her features.

"This scene faded away as the other had done, and I saw the fair woman no more.

"Then it seemed to me that many figures passed and repassed before the window—the wicked woman (as I shall call her to distinguish her), accompanied by a boy the image of herself, whom I knew to be her son. He was apparently older than the fair-haired children, who also passed to and fro, attired as servants, and generally employed in some menial work.

"At last the wicked woman's son, with haughty gestures, ordered the other boy to pick up something that lay on the ground, and when he refused, he raised his cane as though to strike him. Before he could do so, however, the boy flew at him, and they engaged in a fierce struggle.

"In the midst of this the wicked woman, whom I had learned to dread, came forward and separated them; after which she pointed imperiously to the door, and signed to the younger boy to go out.

"He obeyed her mandate, but first threw his arms round his sister in a last embrace, and she detached the pearl necklace from off her neck and gave it to him. He then went out, waving a last adieu to her, and I saw him no more.

"Confused images seemed to crowd before me after this, and I remember nothing clearly until I beheld an infirm and tottering figure led away through the arched doorway, in whom I recognized the tall and stately man I had first seen in company with the wicked woman, but who was now an old man, apparently being supported to his bed to die. As he passed out he laid one trembling hand upon the head of the fair girl, now a blooming woman, and a softer shade came over his face. This the wicked woman noted, and she marked her disapproval by a vindictive frown.

"She also was older-looking, but age had in no degree softened her features; on the contrary, they appeared to me to wear a harsher expression than before.

"In the next scene which came before me, the wicked woman's son was evidently making love to the girl. Both were standing by the old window-seat, but her face was resolutely turned away from him, and when she at last looked at him it was with an expression of uncontrollable horror and dislike.

"Again this scene changed as those before it had done; the young man was gone, and only the light of a grated lantern illumined the room, or rather made darkness visible. The wicked woman was the only occupant of the laundry; she was kneeling by the oaken chest, trying to raise the heavy lid. In her left hand she held a piece of parch-

ment, with large red seals pendent from it. I
knew it to be the old man's will which she was
hiding, thus defrauding the just claimants of their
rights.

"Her hands trembled, and her whole appearance
denoted guilty trepidation. At length, however,
the lid was raised, but just as she was about to replace the parchment in the chest, a figure glided
silently from a dark corner of the window-seat and
confronted her. It was the fair girl, pale, reso-
lute, and extending her hand to claim the will.

"After the first guilty start, which caused her
to drop the parchment into the chest, the wicked
woman hurriedly tried to close the lid. Her
efforts were frustrated, however, by the girl, who
leaned with all her force upon it, keeping it back,
and still held out her hand as before.

"There followed a pause, which seemed to me
very long, but which could in reality have only
lasted a minute.

"It was broken by the wicked woman, who,
hastily casting a glance behind her into the gloom
of the darkened chamber, then seized the girl by
the arm and dragged her with all her force into
the chest. It was but the work of a moment, for
the woman was much the more powerful of the
two, and the poor victim was too much taken by
surprise to make much resistance. I saw one de-
spairing look in her face as her murderess flashed
the lantern before it with a hideous gleam of triumph.

"Then the lid was pressed down upon her, and
I saw no more, only I felt an unutterable terror,
and tried in vain to scream.

"This was not all the vision, however, for before I had mastered my terror the scene was superseded by another.

"This time it was twilight, and the wicked woman and her son were together. The son seemed to be talking eagerly, and grew more and more excited, while the mother stood still and erect, with a malicious smile upon her lips. Presently she moved toward the chest with a fell purpose in her eyes, unlocked it with a key which hung from her girdle, raised the lid and disclosed the contents.

"I understood it all now: the son was asking for the girl whom he had loved, and whom on his return home he missed, and the wicked woman, enraged at hearing for the first time that he had loved her, was determined to have her revenge.

"He should see her again.

"On beholding the dread contents of the chest, the man staggered back horrified; then, doubtless comprehending the case, he turned suddenly upon the murderess, and threw his arm around her, and there ensued a struggle terrible to witness.

"Her proud triumphant glance of malice was now succeeded by one of abject fear, and, as his strength began to gain the mastery, of despair.

"His iron frame heaved for a moment with the violence of his efforts, the next he had forced her down into the chest upon the mouldering body of her victim. I saw her eyes light up with the terror of death for one second, and then her screams were stifled forever beneath the massive lid.

"The horror of this scene was too much for me; I found voice to scream at last, and I suppose it was my cry which alarmed you all."

When Catherine ceased speaking there was a profound silence for a minute, which Mr. Fanshawe was the first to break as he said with a peculiar intonation in his voice, "It is very strange, very unaccountable," reëchoing all our thoughts.

Now it happened that Mr. Fleet, our family lawyer, was among our guests that Christmastime, and since the discovery of the chest and bones had taken a great interest in the whole affair. He now questioned and cross-questioned Catherine, and seemed quite satisfied with the result.

"This would have made a fine case," said he, "if only it had been a question of the right of succession, for any lawyer to make out; but unfortunately the events are too long past to have any bearing upon the present." (There Mr. Fleet was wrong, though we none of us knew it at the time.)

We now all launched forth into conjectures and opinions, during which Catherine lay still and weary upon the sofa. I saw this, and thought it quite time to put an end to the day's adventures by suggesting a retirement for the night, and we were soon all dispersed to dream of the mysterious vision and discovery.

I think we were none of us sorry when morning dawned without any further tragedy (by *us*, I mean the female part of the establishment).

When I came down to breakfast I found Mr. Fleet very active on the subject of the night before.

"A surgeon ought to be immediately sent for to pronounce an opinion on the contents of the chest," he said; and Dr. Driscoll presently came, and after examining the bones minutely, decided that they were, as we thought, those of two females, who might have been from one to two hundred years dead.

Mr. Fleet next offered to decipher the will, for such he imagined the parchment to be, and he and Mr. Fanshawe were closeted together for some time.

When they at last appeared again, they looked much interested and excited, and led me away to inform me of the result of their examination.

They told me that the document had proved to be a will, but that there was a circumstance connected with it which greatly added to the mystery of the whole business. This was the mention of the name of L'Estrange. I was, of course, as much surprised as they, and heard the will read with great interest.

I cannot remember the technical terms in which it was expressed. Mr. Fleet read me the translation he had made, for the original was in old English; but it was to this effect:

It purported to be the will of Reginald, Viscount St. Aubyn, in which he bequeathed all his inheritance to his lawful son Francis St. Aubyn—commonly known by the name of Francis l'Estrange—and to his heirs forever. It was signed Reginald, Viscount St. Aubyn, and the witnesses were John Murray and Phœbe Brett, who in the old copy had each affixed their mark.

Mr. Fleet affirmed that it was a perfectly legal document, but this was not all it contained.

There was an appendix which our lawyer translated as follows:

"In order to avoid all disputes and doubts which might otherwise arise, I do hereby declare that my lawful wife was Editha, youngest daughter of Francis l'Estrange, Baronet, and that the register of our marriage may·be seen in the church of St. Andrew, Haslet. By this marriage we had two children, a son Francis, and a daughter Catherine, commonly called Francis and Catherine l'Estrange. And I hereby declare that Agatha Thornhaugh was not legally married to me as she imagined, my lawful wife being alive at the time; neither do I leave to her son by her first husband, Ralph Thornhaugh, any part or share in my inheritance."

Both the will and the writing at the foot of it were dated the 14th of May, 1668.

This accumulation of mysteries caused me for a time to feel quite bewildered and unable to think, but Mr. Fleet was in his element.

"Here is a case worth entering into," said he, and he further went on to state that he had no doubt that the L'Estranges mentioned in the will were our Catherine's ancestors, the Christian names being similar rendering it more than probable. She was most likely a direct descendant of Francis l'Estrange, the heir mentioned in the will, who was no doubt also the fair-haired boy Catherine had seen in her vision.

The bones were those of his sister, the murdered Catherine l'Estrange, and of her murderess Agatha Thornhaugh, herself immured by her own son; but the matter ought not to rest on mere surmise, and the first place to go to for corroborating evidence was Craymoor church.

The rapidity with which Mr. Fleet came to his

conclusions increased my bewilderment, and I was at a loss to know what evidence he expected to gain from Craymoor church. He reminded me, however, of Catherine's statement that "the wicked woman" of her vision resembled the effigy on the monument there.

Thither, then, the lawyer repaired, accompanied by Mr. Fanshawe and George. It was thought best to keep the sequel of the story from Catherine and the others until it was explained more fully, as Mr. Fleet boldly affirmed it should be.   I awaited anxiously the result of their researches, and they exceeded I think even our good investigator's hopes.

Not only had they deciphered the inscription round the old monument, but with leave from the clergyman and the assistance of the sexton they had disinterred the coffin and found it to be filled with stones.

I am aware that this was rather an illegal proceeding, but as Mr. Fleet was only acting *en amateur* and not professionally, he did not stick at trifles.

The inscription was in Latin, and stated that the tomb was erected in memory of Agatha, wife of Reginald, Viscount St. Aubyn, who was buried beneath, and who died on the 31st day of December, 1649—exactly two hundred years before the day on which Catherine had seen the vision.

I could not help thinking it shocking that the villagers had for two centuries been worshipping in the presence of a perpetual lie, but Mr. Fleet thought only of the grand corroboration of his "case."   He applied to Mr. Fanshawe to take the next step, namely, to write to Catherine's aunt

and only living relative, to tell her the whole story,
and beg her to assist in elucidating matters by
giving all the information she could respecting the
L'Estrange family.

This was done, and we anxiously awaited the
answer. Meantime, all my guests were clamorous
to hear the contents of the will, and I had to ap-
pease them as best I could, by promising that they
should know all soon.

In a few days, old Miss l'Estrange's answer
came. She said her brother, father, and grand-
father had all served in India, and that she believed her great-grandfather, who was a Francis
l'Estrange, to have passed most of his life abroad,
there having been a cloud over his early youth.
What this was, however, she could not say. She
affirmed that the L'Estranges had in old times resided in ——shire; and she further stated that her
father's family had consisted of herself and her
brother, whose only child Catherine was.

This was certainly not much information, but it
was enough for our purpose. We no longer remained in doubt as to the truth of Mr. Fleet's ver-
sion of the story, and when he himself told it to
all our family-party one evening, every one agreed
that he had certainly succeeded in making out a
very clever case.

As for Catherine, on being told that the figures
she had beheld in the vision were thought to be
those of her ancestors, she was not so much surprised as I expected, but said that she had had a
presentiment all along that the tragedies she had
witnessed were in some way connected with her
own family.

I must not forget to say that on ascertaining that the parish church of Haslet was still standing, we searched the register, and another link of evidence was made clear by the finding of the looked-for entry.

There remains little more to be told. The charge of the old will was committed to Mr. Fleet, and Catherine's story has been carefully laid up among the archives of our family. I say advisedly of *our* family, for the line of the L'Estranges, alias St. Aubyns, has been united to ours by the marriage of Catherine to my son George, which took place in 1850.

I who write this am an old woman now, but I still live with my son and daughter-in-law.

George has bought Craymoor Grange, thus rendering justice after the lapse of two centuries, and restoring the inheritance of her fathers to the rightful owner.

I have but one more incident to relate, and I have done. A short time ago, old Miss l'Estrange died, bequeathing all her worldly possessions to Catherine. Among these were some old family relics. Catherine was looking over them as George unpacked them, and she presently came to a miniature of a young and beautiful girl with fair hair and blue eyes, and a wistful expression, and with it a necklace of pearls strung in a diamond pattern. On seeing these she became suddenly grave, and handing them to me, said: "They are the same; the young girl, and the pearl necklace I told you of." No more was said at the time, for the children were present, and we had always avoided alluding to the horrible family tragedy before

them; but if we had still retained any doubt about
its truth—which we had not—this would have set
it at rest.

If you were to visit Craymoor Grange now, you
would find no old laundry. The part of the house
containing it has been pulled down, and children
play and chickens peckett on the ground where it
once stood.

The oaken chest has also long since been destroyed.

HAUNTED.

HAUNTED.

SOME few years ago one of those great national conventions which draw together all ages and conditions of the sovereign people of America was held in Charleston, South Carolina.

Colonel Demariou, one of the State Representatives, had attended that great national convention; and, after an exciting week, was returning home, having a long and difficult journey before him.

A pair of magnificent horses, attached to a light buggy, flew merrily enough over a rough-country for a while; but toward evening stormy weather reduced the roads to a dangerous conditon, and compelled the Colonel to relinquish his purpose of reaching home that night, and to stop at a small wayside tavern, whose interior, illuminated by blazing wood-fires, spread a glowing halo among the dripping trees as he approached it, and gave promise of warmth and shelter at least.

Drawing up to this modest dwelling, Colonel Demarion saw through its uncurtained windows that there was no lack of company within. Beneath the trees, too, an entanglement of rustic vehicles, giving forth red gleams from every dripping angle, told him that beasts as well as men were cared for. At the open door appeared the form of a man, who, at the sound of wheels, but not seeing

115

in the outside darkness whom he addressed, called out, "'Tain't no earthly use a-stoppin' here."

Caring more for his chattels than for himself, the Colonel paid no further regard to this address than to call loudly for the landlord.

At the tone of authority, the man in outline more civilly announced himself to be the host; yet so far from inviting the traveller to alight, insisted that the house was "as full as it could pack;" but that there was a place a little farther down the road where the gentleman would be certain to find excellent accommodation.

"What stables have you here?" demanded the traveller, giving no more heed to this than to the former announcement; but bidding his servant to alight, and preparing to do so himself.

"Stables!" repeated the baffled host, shading his eyes so as to scrutinize the newcomer, "*stables,* Cap'n?"

"Yes, *stables.* I want you to take care of my horses; *1* can take care of myself. Some shelter for cattle you must have by the look of these traps," pointing to the wagons. "I don't want my horses to be kept standing out in this storm, you know."

"No, Major. Why no, certn'y; Marion's ain't over a mile, and——"

"Conf—!" muttered the Colonel; "but it's over the *river,* which I don't intend to ford to-night under any consideration."

So saying, the Colonel leaped to the ground, directing his servant to cover the horses and then get out his valise; while the host, thus defeated, assumed the best grace he could to say that he would see what could be done "for the *horses.*"

"I am a soldier, my man," added the Colonel in a milder tone, as he stamped his cold feet on the porch and shook off the rain from his traveling-gear; "I am used to rough fare and a hard couch: all we want is shelter. A corner of the floor will suffice for me and my rug; a private room I can dispense with at such times as these."

The landlord seemed no less relieved at this assurance than mollified by the explanation of a traveller whom he now saw was of a very different stamp from those who usually frequented the tavern. "For the matter of *stables*, his were newly put up, and first-rate," he said; and "cert'n'y the Gen'ral was welcome to a seat by the fire while 'twas a-storming so fierce."

Colonel Demarion gave orders to his servant regarding the horses, while the landlord, kicking at what seemed to be a bundle of sacking down behind the door, shouted—"Jo! Ho, Jo! Wake up, you sleepy-headed nigger! Be alive, boy, and show this gentleman's horses to the stables." Upon a repetition of which charges a tall, gaunt, dusky figure lifted itself from out of the dark corner, and grew taller and more gaunt as it stretched itself into waking with a grin which was the most visible part of it, by reason of two long rows of ivory gleaming in the red glare. The hard words had fallen as harmless on Jo's ear-drum as the kicks upon his impassive frame. To do Jo's master justice, the kicks were not vicious kicks, and the rough language was but an intimation that dispatch was needed. Very much of the spaniel's nature had Jo; and as he rolled along the passage to fetch a lantern, his mouth expanded into a still broader

grin at the honor of attending so stately a gentleman. Quick, like his master, too, was Jo to dis-
criminate between "real gentlefolks" and the
"white trash" whose rough-coated, rope-harnessed
mules were the general occupants of his stables.

"Splendid pair, sir," said the now conciliating
landlord. "Shove some o' them mules out into the
shed, Jo (which your horses 'll feel more to hum
in my new stalls, Gen'ral).

Again cautioning his man Plato not to leave them
one moment, Colonel Demarion turned to enter the
house.

"You'll find a rough crowd in here, sir," said the
host, as he paused on the threshold; "but a good
fire, anyhow. 'Tain't many of these loafers as
understand this convention business—I *presume*,
Gen'ral, you've attended the convention—they all
on 'em *thinks* they does, tho'. Fact most on 'em
thinks they'd orter be on the committee theirselves.
Good many on 'em is from Char'ston to-day, but is
in the same fix as yerself, Gen'ral—can't get across
the river to-night."

"I see, I see," cried the statesman, with a gesture
toward the sitting-room. "Now what have you got
in your larder, Mr. Landlord? and send some supper out to my servant; he must make a bed of the
carriage-mats to-night."

The landlord introduced his guest into a room
filled chiefly with that shiftless and noxious element of Southern society known as "mean whites."
Pipes and drinks, and excited arguments, engaged
these people as they stood or sat in groups. The
host addressed those who were gathered round the
log-fire, and they opened a way for the new-comer,

some few, with republican freedom, inviting him to be seated, the rest giving one furtive glance, and then, in antipathy born of envy, skulking away.

The furniture of this comfortless apartment consisted of sloppy, much-jagged deal tables, dirty whittled benches, and a few uncouth chairs. The walls were dirty with accumulated tobacco stains, and so moist and filthy was the floor, that the sound only of scraping seats and heavy footsteps told that it was of boards and not bare earth.

Seated with his back toward the majority of the crowd, and shielded by his newspaper, Colonel Demarion sat awhile unobserved; but was presently recognized by a man from his own immediate neighborhood, when the information was quickly whispered about that no less a person than their distinguished Congressman was among them.

This piece of news speedily found its way to the ears of the landlord, to whom Colonel Demarion was known by name only, and forthwith he reappeared to overwhelm the representative of his State with apologies for the uncourteous reception which had been given him, and to express his now very sincere regrets that the house offered no suitable accommodation for the gentleman. Satisfied as to the safety of his chattels, the Colonel generously dismissed the idea of having anything either to resent or to forgive; and assured the worthy host that' he would accept of no exclusive indulgences.

In spite of which the landlord bustled about to bring in a separate table, on which he spread a clean coarse cloth, and a savory supper of broiled ham, hot corncakes, and coffee; every few minutes stopping to renew his apologies, and even appear-

ing to grow confidentially communicative regarding
his domestic economies; until the hungry traveller
cut him short with "Don't say another word about
it, my friend; you have not a spare sleeping-room,
and that is enough.   Find me a corner—a clean
corner"— looking round upon the most unclean
corners of that room—"perhaps up-stairs some-.
where, and——"

"Ah! *upsta'rs*, Gen'ral.   Now, that's jest what
I had in my mind to ax you.   Fact is ther' *is* a
spar' room upsta'rs, as comfortable a room as the
best of folks can wish; but——"

"But it's crammed with sleeping folks, so there's
an end of it," cried the senator, thoroughly bored.

"No, sir, ain't no person in it; and ther' ain't
no person likely to be in it 'cept 'tis *yerself*, Colonel Demarion.   Leastways——"

After a good deal of hesitation and embarrass-
ment, the host, in mysterious whispers, imparted
the startling fact that this most desirable sleeping
room was *haunted;* that the injury he had sustained
in consequence had compelled him to fasten it up
altogether; that he had come to be very suspicious
of admitting strangers, and had limited his custom
of late to what the bar could supply, keeeping the
matter hushed up in the hope that it might be the
sooner forgotten by the neighbors; but that in the
case of Colonel Demarion he had now made bold to
mention it; "as I can't but think, sir," he urged,
"you'd find it prefer'ble to sleepin' on the floor or
sittin' up all night along ov these loafers.   Fer if
'tis any deceivin' trick got up in the house, maybe
they won't try it on, sir, to a gentleman of your
reputation,"

Colonel Demarion became interested in the landlord's confidences, but could only gather in further
explanation that for some time past all travellers
who had occupied that room had "made off in the
middle of the night, never showin' their faces at
the inn again;" that on endeavoring to arrest one
or more in their nocturnal flight, they—all more or
less terrified—had insisted on escaping without a
moment's delay, assigning no other reason than
that they had seen a ghost. "Not that folks seem
to get much harm by it, Colonel—not by the
way they makes off without paying a cent of
money!"

Great indeed was the satisfaction evinced by the
victim of unpaid bills on the Colonel's declaring
that the haunted chamber was the very room for
him. "If to be turned out of my bed at midnight
is all I have to fear, we will see who comes off master in my case. So, Mr. Landlord, let the chamber
be got ready directly, and have a good fire built
there at once."

The exultant host hurried away to confide the
great news to Jo, and with him to make the necessary preparations. "Come what will, Jo, Colonel
Demarion ain't the man to make off without paying down good money for his accommodations."

In reasonable time, Colonel Demarion was
beckoned out of the public room, and conducted
up-stairs by the landlord, who, after receiving a
cheerful "good-night," paused on the landing to
hear his guest bolt and bar the door within, and
then push a piece of furniture against it. "Ah,"
murmured the host, as a sort of misgiving came
over him, "if a apparishum has a mind to come

thar, 'tain't all the bolts and bars in South Carolina as 'll kip'en away."

But the Colonel's precaution of securing his door,
as also that of placing his revolvers in readiness,
had not the slightest reference to the reputed ghost.
Spiritual disturbances of such kind he feared not.
Spirits *tangible* were already producing ominous
demonstrations in the rooms below, nor was it possible to conjecture what troubles these might evolve.
Glad enough to escape from the noisy company, he
took a survey of his evil-reputed chamber. The
only light was that of the roaring, crackling, blazing wood-fire, and no other was needed. And what
storm-benighted traveller, when fierce winds and
rains are lashing around his lodging, can withstand
the cheering influences of a glorious log-fire? especially if, as in that wooden tenement, that fire be of
abundant pine-knots. It rivals the glare of gas and
the glow of a furnace; it charms away the musti-
ness and fustiness of years, and causes all that is
dull and dead around to laugh and dance in its
bright light.

By the illumination of just such a fire, Colonel
Demarion observed that the apartment offered nothing worthier of remark than that the furniture was
superior to anything that might be expected in a
small wayside tavern. In truth, the landlord had
expended a considerable sum in fitting up this, his
finest chamber, and had therefore sufficient reason
to bemoan its unprofitableness.

Having satisfied himself as to his apparent secur-
ity, the senator thought no more of spirits palpable
or impalpable; but to the far graver issues of the
convention his thoughts reverted. It was yet

early; he lighted a cigar, and in full appreciation of his retirement, took out his note-book and plunged into the affairs of state. Now and then he was recalled to the circumstances of his situation by the swaggering tread of unsteady feet about the house, or when the boisterous shouts below raged above the outside storm; but even then he only glanced up from his papers to congratulate himself upon his agreeable seclusion.

Thus he sat for above an hour, then he heaped fresh logs upon the hearth, looked again to his revolvers, and retired to rest.

The house-clock was striking twelve as the Colonel awoke. He awoke suddenly from a sound sleep, flashing, as it were, into full consciousness, his mind and memory clear, all his faculties invigorated, his ideas undisturbed, but with a perfect conviction that he was not alone.

He lifted his head. A man was standing a few feet from the bed, and between it and the fire, which was still burning, and burning brightly enough to display every object in the room, and to define the outline of the intruder clearly. His dress also and his features were plainly distinguishable: the dress was a travelling-costume, in fashion somewhat out of date; the features wore a mournful and distressed expression—the eyes were fixed upon the Colonel. The right arm hung down, and the hand, partially concealed, might, for aught the Colonel knew, be grasping one of his own revolvers; the left arm was folded against the waist. The man seemed about to advance still closer to the bed, and returned the occupant's gaze with a fixed stare.

"Stand, or I'll fire!" cried the Colonel, taking

in all this at a glance, and starting up in his bed, revolver in hand.

The man remained still.

"What is your business here?" demanded the statesman, thinking he was addressing one of the roughs from below.

The man was silent.

"Leave this room, if you value your life," shouted the indignant soldier, pointing his revolver.

The man was motionless.

"RETIRE! or by heaven I'll send a bullet through you!"

But the man moved not an inch.

The Colonel fired. The bullet lodged in the breast of the stranger, but he started not. The soldier leaped to the floor and fired again. The shot entered the heart, pierced the body, and lodged in the wall beyond; and the Colonel beheld the hole where the bullet had entered, and the firelight glimmering through it. And yet the intruder stirred not. Astounded, the Colonel dropped his revolver, and stood face to face before the unmoved man.

"Colonel Demarion," spake the deep solemn voice of the perforated stranger, "in vain you shoot me—I am dead already."

The soldier, with all his bravery, gasped, spellbound. The firelight gleamed through the hole in the body, and the eyes of the shooter were riveted there.

"Fear nothing," spake the mournful presence; "I seek but to divulge my wrongs. Until my death shall be avenged my unquiet spirit lingers here. Listen,"

Speechless, motionless was the statesman; and the mournful apparition thus slowly and distinctly continued:

"Four years ago I travelled with one I trusted. We lodged here. That night my comrade murdered me. He plunged a dagger into my heart while I slept. He covered the wound with a plaster. He feigned to mourn my death. He told the people here I had died of heart complaint; that I had long been ailing. I had gold and treasures. With my treasure secreted beneath his garments he paraded mock grief at my grave. Then he departed. In distant parts he sought to forget his crime; but his stolen gold brought him only the curse of an evil conscience. Rest and peace are not for him. He now prepares to leave his native land forever. Under an assumed name that man is this night in Charleston. In a few hours he will sail for Europe. Colonel Demarion, you must prevent it. Justice and humanity demand that a murderer roam not at large, nor squander more of the wealth that is by right my children's."

The spirit paused. To the extraordinary revelation the Colonel had listened in rapt astonishment. He gazed at the presence, at the firelight glimmering through it—through the very place where a human heart would be—and he felt that he was indeed in the presence of a supernatural being. He thought of the landlord's story; but while earnestly desiring to sift the truth of the mystery, words refused to come to his aid.

"Do you hesitate?" said the mournful spirit. "Will *you* also flee, when my orphan children cry for retribution?" Seeming to anticipate the will of the Colonel, "I await your promise, senator," he said. "There is no time to lose."

With a mighty effort, the South Carolinian said, "I promise. What would you have me do?"

In the same terse, solemn manner, the ghostly visitor gave the real and assumed names of the murderer, described his person and dress at the present time, described a certain curious ring he was then wearing, together with other distinguishing characteristics: all being carefully noted down by Colonel Demarion, who, by degrees, recovered his self-possession, and pledged himself to use every endeavor to bring the murderer to justice.

Then, with a portentous wave of the hand, "It is well," said the apparition. "Not until the spirit of my murderer shall be separated from the mortal clay can *my* spirit rest in peace." And vanished.

Half-past six in the morning was the appointed time for the steamer to leave Charleston; and the Colonel lost not a moment in preparing to depart. As he hurried down the stairs he encountered the landlord, who—his eyes rolling in terror—made an attempt to speak. Unheeding, except to demand his carriage, the Colonel pushed past him, and effected a quick escape toward the back premises, shouting lustily for "Jo" and "Plato," and for his carriage to be got ready immediately. A few minutes more, and the bewildered host was recalled to the terrible truth by the noise of the carriage dashing through the yard and away down the road; and it was some miles nearer Charleston before the unfortunate man ceased to peer after it in the darkness—as if by so doing he could recover damages—and bemoan to Jo the utter ruin of his house and hopes.

Thirty miles of hard driving had to be accomplished in little more than five hours. No great achievement under favorable circumstances; but the horses were only half refreshed from their yesterday's journey, and though the storm was over, the roads were in a worse condition than ever.

Colonel Demarion resolved to be true to his promise; and fired by a curiosity to investigate the extraordinary communication which had been revealed to him, urged on his horses, and reached the wharf at Charleston just as the steamer was being loosed from her moorings.

He hailed her. "Stop her! Business with the captain! STOP HER!"

Her machinery was already in motion; her iron lungs were puffing forth dense clouds of smoke and steam; and as the Colonel shouted—the crowd around, from sheer delight in shouting, echoing his "Stop her! stop her!"—the voices on land were confounded with the voices of the sailors, the rattling of chains, and the haulings of ropes.

Among the passengers standing to wave farewells to their friends on the wharf were some who recognised Colonel Demarion, and drew the captain's attention toward him; and as he continued vehemently to gesticulate, that officer, from his post of observation, demanded the nature of the business which should require the ship's detention. Already the steamer was clear of the wharf. In another minute she might be beyond each of the voice; therefore, failing by gestures and entreaties to convince the captain of the importance of his errand, Colonel Demarion, in desperation, cried at the top of his voice, "A murderer on board! For God's

sake, STOP!" He wished to have made this startling
declaration in private, but not a moment was to
be lost; and the excitement around him was
intense.

In the midst of the confusion another cry of
"Man overboard!" might have been heard in a distant part of the ship, had not the attention of the
crowd been fastened on the Colonel. Such a cry
was, however, uttered, offering a still more urgent
motive for stopping; and the steamer being again
made fast, Colonel Demarion was received on
board.

"Let not a soul leave the vessel!" was his first
and prompt suggestion; and the order being issued
he drew the captain aside, and concisely explained
his grave commission. The captain thereupon conducted him to his private room, and summoned the
steward, before whom the details were given, and
the description of the murderer was read over.
The steward, after considering attentively, seemed
inclined to associate the description with that of a
passenger whose remarkably dejected appearance
had already attracted his observation. In such a
grave business it was, however, necessary to proceed with the utmost caution, and the "passenger-
book" was produced. Upon reference to its pages,
the three gentlemen were totally dismayed by
the discovery that the name of this same dejected
individual was that under which, according to
the apparition, the murderer had engaged his
passage.

"I am here to charge that man with murder,"
said Colonel Demarion. "He must be arrested."

Horrified as the captain was at this astounding

declaration, yet, on account of the singular and unusual mode by which the Colonel had become possessed of the facts, and the impossibility of proving
the charge, he hesitated in consenting to the arrest
of a passenger. The steward proposed that they
should repair to the saloons and deck, and while
conversing with one or another of the passengers,
mention—as it were casually—in the hearing of the
suspected party his own proper name, and observe
the effect produced on him. To this they agreed,
and without loss of time joined the passengers,
assigning some feasible cause for a short delay of
the ship.

The saloon was nearly empty, and while the
steward went below, the other two repaired to the
deck, where they observed a crowd gathered sea-
ward, apparently watching something over the
ship's side.

During the few minutes which had detained the
captain in this necessarily hurried business, a boat
had been lowered, and some sailors had put off in
her to rescue the person who was supposed to have
fallen overboard; and it was only now, on joining
the crowd, that the captain learned the particulars
of the accident. "Who was it?" "What was he
like?" they exclaimed simultaneously. That a
man had fallen overboard was all that could be ascertained. Some one had seen him run across the
deck, looking wildly about him. A splash in the
water had soon afterward attracted attention to the
spot, and a body had since been seen struggling on
the surface. The waves were rough after the
storm, and thick with seaweed, and the sailors had
as yet missed the body. The two gentlemen took

9

their post among the watchers, and kept their eyes
intently upon the waves, and upon the sailors bat-
tling against them. Ere long they see the body
rise again to the surface. Floated on a powerful
wave, they can for the few moments breathlessly
scrutinize it. The color of the dress is observed.
A face of agony upturned displays a peculiar con-
tour of forehead; the hair, the beard; and now he
struggles—an arm is thrown up, and a remarkable
ring catches the Colonel's eye. "Great heavens!
The whole description tallies!" The sailors pull
hard for the spot, the next stroke and they will
rescue——

A monster shark is quicker than they. The sea
is tinged with blood. The man is no more!

Shocked and silent, Colonel Demarion and the
captain quitted the deck and resummoned the steward, who had, but without success, visited the berths
and various parts of the ship for the individual in
question. Every hole and corner was now, by the
captain's order carefully searched, but in vain; and
as no further information concerning the missing
party could be obtained, and the steward persisted
in his statement regarding his general appearance,
they proceeded to examine his effects. In these
he was identified beyond a doubt. Papers and
relics proved not only his guilt but his remorse;
remorse which, as the apparition had said, permitted him no peace in his wanderings.

Those startling words, "A murderer on board!"
had doubtless struck fresh terror to his heart and,
unable to face the accusation, he had thus termi-
nated his wretched existence.

Colonel Demarion revisited the little tavern, and

on several occasions occupied the haunted chamber;
but never again had he the honor of receiving a midnight commission from a ghostly visitor, and never
again had the landlord to bemoan the flight of a
non-paying customer.

PICHON & SONS, OF THE CROIX ROUSSE.

PICHON & SONS, OF THE CROIX ROUSSE.

GIRAUDIER, *pharmacien, première classe,* is the legend, recorded in huge, ill-proportioned letters, which directs the attention of the stranger to the most prosperous-looking shop in the grand *place* of La Croix Rousse, a well-known suburb of the beautiful city of Lyons, which has its share of the shabby gentility and poor pretence common to the suburban commerce of great towns.

Giraudier is not only *pharmacien* but *propriétaire,* though not by inheritance; his possession of one of the prettiest and most prolific of the small vineyards in the beautiful suburb, and a charming inconvenient house, with low ceilings, liliputian bedrooms, and a, profusion of *persiennes, jalousies,* and *contrevents,* comes by purchase. This enviable little *terre* was sold by the Nation, when that terrible abstraction transacted the public business of France; and it was bought very cheaply by the strong-minded father of the Giraudier of the present, who was not disturbed by the evil reputation which the place had gained, at a time the peasants of France, having been bullied into a renunciation of religion, eagerly cherished superstition. The Giraudier of the present cherishes the particular superstition in question affectionately; it reminds him of an uncommonly good bargain made in his favor, which is

always a pleasant association of ideas, especially to
a Frenchman, still more especially to a Lyonnais;
and it attracts strangers to his *pharmacie*, and leads
to transactions in *Grand Chartreuse* and *Crême de
Roses*, ensuing naturally on the narration of the history of Pichon & Sons. Giraudier is not of aristocratic principles and sympathies; on the contrary,
he has decided republican leanings, and considers
Le Progrès a masterpiece of journalistic literature;
but, as he says simply and strongly, " it is not because a man is a marquis that one is not to keep
faith with him; a bad action is not good because it
harms a good-for-nothing of a noble; the more
when that good-for-nothing is no longer a noble,
but *pour rire."* At the easy price of acquiescence
in these sentiments, the stranger hears one of the
most authentic, best-remembered, most popular of
the many traditions of the bad old times " before
General Bonaparte," as Giraudier, who has no
sympathy with any later designation of *le grand
homme,* calls the Emperor, whose statue one can
perceive—a speck in the distance—from the threshold of the *pharmacie.*

The Marquis de Sénanges, in the days of the triumph of the great Revolution, was fortunate enough
to be out of France, and wise enough to remain away
from that country, though he persisted, long after
the old *régime* was as dead as the Ptolemies, in believing it merely suspended, and the Revolution a
lamentable accident of vulgar complexion, but happily temporary duration. The Marquis de Sénanges, who affected the *style régence,* and was the
politest of infidels and the most refined of voluptu-
aries, got on indifferently in inappreciative foreign

parts; but the members of his family — his brother and sisters, two of whom were guillotined, while the third escaped to Savoy and found refuge there in a convent of her order—got on exceedingly ill in France. If the *ci-devant* Marquis had had plenty of money to expend in such feeble imitations of his accustomed pleasures as were to be had out of Paris, he would not have been much affected by the fate of his relatives. But money became exceedingly scarce; the Marquis had actually beheld many of his peers reduced to the necessity of earning the despicable but indispensable article after many ludicrous fashions. And the duration of this absurd upsetting of law, order, privilege, and property began to assume unexpected and very unpleasant proportions.

The Château de Sénanges, with its surrounding lands, was confiscated to the Nation, during the third year of the "emigration" of the Marquis de Sénanges; and the greater part of the estate was purchased by a thrifty, industrious, and rich *avocat*, named Prosper Alix, a widower with an only daughter. Prosper Alix enjoyed the esteem of the entire neighborhood. First, he was rich; secondly, he was of a taciturn disposition, and of a neutral tint in politics. He had done well under the old *régime* and, he was doing well under the new— thank God, or the Supreme Being, or the First Cause, or the goddess Reason herself, for all;—he would have invoked Dagon, Moloch, or Kali, quite as readily as the Saints and the Madonna, who has gone so utterly out of fashion of late. Nobody was afraid to speak out before Prosper Alix; he was not a spy; and though a cold-hearted man, except in the instance of his only daughter, he never harmed anybody.

Very likely it was because he was the last person in the vicinity whom anybody would have suspected of being applied to by the dispossessed family, that the son of the Marquis' brother, a young man of promise, of courage, of intellect, and of morals of decidedly a higher calibre than those actually and tradionally imputed to the family, sought the aid of the new possessor of the Château de Sénanges, which had changed its old title for that of the Maison Alix. The father of M. Paul de Sénanges had perished in the September massacres; his mother had been guillotined at Lyons; and he—who had been saved by the interposition of a young comrade, whose father had, in the wonderful rotations of the wheel of Fate, acquired authority in the place where he had once esteemed the notice of the nephew of the Marquis a crowning honor for his son—had passed through the common vicissitudes of that dreadful time, which would take a volume for their recital in each individual instance.

Paul de Sénanges was a handsome young fellow, frank, high-spirited, and of a brisk and happy temperament; which, however, modified by the many misfortunes he had undergone, was not permanently changed. He had plenty of capacity for enjoyment in him still; and as his position was very isolated, and his mind had become enlightened on social and political matters to an extent in which the men of his family would have discovered utter degradation and the women diabolical possession, he would not have been very unhappy if, under the

new condition of things, he could have lived in his
native country and gained an honest livelihood.
But he could not do that, he was too thoroughly
"suspect;" the antecedents of his family were too
powerful against him: his only chance would have
been to have gone into the popular camp as an extreme, violent partisan, to have out-Heroded the
revolutionary Herods; and that Paul de Sénanges
was too honest to do. So he was reduced to being
thankful that he had escaped with his life, and to
watching for an opportunity of leaving France and
gaining some country where the reign of liberty,
fraternity, and equality was not quite so oppressive.

The long-looked-for opportunity at length offered
itself, and Paul de Sénanges was instructed by his
uncle the Marquis that he must contrive to reach
Marseilles, whence he should be transported to
Spain—in which country the illustrious emigrant
was then residing—by a certain named date. His
uncle's communication arrived safely, and the plan
proposed seemed a secure and eligible one. Only
in two respects was it calculated to make Paul de
Sénanges thoughtful. The first was, that his uncle
should take any interest in the matter of his safety;
the second, what could be the nature of a certain
deposit which the Marquis's letter directed him to
procure, if possible, from the Château de Sénanges.
The fact of this injunction explained, in some measure, the first of the two difficulties. It was plain
that whatever were the contents of this packet which
he was to seek for, according to the indications
marked on a ground-plan drawn by his uncle and
enclosed in the letter, the Marquis wanted them,
and could not procure them except by the agency

of his nephew. That the Marquis should venture to direct Paul de Sénanges to put himself in communication with Prosper Alix, would have been surprising to any one acquainted only with the external and generally understood features of the character of the new proprietor of the Château de Sénanges. But a few people knew Prosper Alix thoroughly, and the Marquis was one of the number; he was keen enough to know in theory that, in the case of a man with only one weakness, that is likely to be a very weak weakness indeed, and to apply the theory to the *avocat*. The beautiful, pious, and aristocratic mother of Paul de Sénanges —a lady to whose superiority the Marquis had rendered the distinguished testimony of his dislike, not hesitating to avow that she was "much too good for *his* taste"—had been very fond of, and very kind to, the motherless daughter of Prosper Alix, and he held her memory in reverence which he accorded to nothing beside, human or divine, and taught his daughter the matchless worth of the friend she had lost. The Marquis knew this, and though he had little sympathy with the sentiment, he believed he might use it in the present instance to his own profit, with safety. The event proved that he was right. Private negotiations, with the manner of whose transaction we are not concerned, passed between the *avocat* and the *ci-devant* Marquis; and the young man, then leading a life in which skulking had a large share, in the vicinity of Dijon, was instructed to present himself at the Maison Alix, under the designation of Henri Glaire, and in the character of an artist in house-decoration. The circumstances of his life in childhood and boyhood had led to his being almost safe from recognition as a man at Lyons; and, indeed, all the people on the *ci-devant* visiting-list of the château had been pretty nearly killed off, in the noble and patriotic ardor of the revolutionary times.

The ancient Château de Sénanges was proudly placed near the summit of the "Holy Hill," and had suffered terrible depredations when the church at Fourvières was sacked, and the shrine desecrated with that ingenious impiety which is characteristic of the French; but it still retained somewhat of its former heavy grandeur. The château was much too large for the needs, tastes, or ambition of its present owner, who was too wise, if even he had been of an ostentatious disposition, not to have sedulously resisted its promptings. The jealousy of the nation of brothers was easily excited, and departure from simplicity and frugality was apt to be commented upon by domiciliary visits, and the eager imposition of fanciful fines. That portion of the vast building occupied by Prosper Alix and the *citoyenne* Berthe, his daughter, presented an appearance of well-to-do comfort and modest ease, which contrasted with the grandiose proportions and the elaborate decorations of the wide corridors, huge flat staircases, and lofty panelled apartments. The *avocat* and his daughter lived quietly in the old place, hoping, after a general fashion, for better times, but not finding the present very bad; the father becoming day by day more pleasant with his bargain, the daughter growing fonder of the great house, and the noble *bocages*, of the scrappy little vineyards, struggling for existence on the sunny hill-side, and the place where the famous shrine

had been. They had done it much damage; they
had parted its riches among them; the once ever-
open doors were shut, and the worn flags were un-
trodden; but nothing could degrade it, nothing could
destroy what had been, in the mind of Berthe Alix,
who was as devout as her father was unconcernedly
unbelieving. Berthe was wonderfully well educated
for a Frenchwoman of that period, and surprisingly
handsome for a Frenchwoman of any. Not too tall
to offend the taste of her compatriots, and not too
short to be dignified and graceful, she had a symmetrical figure, and a small, well-poised head,
whose profuse, shining, silken dark-brown hair she
wore as nature intended, in a shower of curls, never
touched by the hand of the coiffeur,—curls which
clustered over her brow, and fell far down on her
shapely neck. Her features were fine; the eyes
very dark, and the mouth very red; the complexion
clear and rather pale, and the style of the face and
its expression lofty. When Berthe Alix was a
child, people were accustomed to say she was pretty
and refined enough to belong to the aristocracy;
nobody would have dared to say so now, prettiness
and refinement, together with all the other virtues
admitted to a place on the patriotic roll, having
become national property.

Berthe loved her father dearly. She was deeply
impressed with the sense of her supreme importance
to him, and fully comprehended that he would be
influenced by and through her when all other persuasion or argument would be unavailing. When
Prosper Alix wished and intended to do anything
rather mean or selfish, he did it without letting
Berthe know; and when he wished to leave undone

something which he knew his daughter would decide ought to be done, he carefully concealed from her the existence of the dilemma. Nevertheless, this system did not prevent the father and daughter being very good and even confidential friends. Prosper Alix loved his daughter immeasurably, and respected her more than he respected any one in the world. With regard to her persevering religiousness, when such things were not only out of fashion and date, but illegal as well, he was very tolerant. Of course it was weak, and an absurdity; but every woman, even his beautiful, incomparable Berthe, was weak and absurd on some point or other; and, after all, he had come to the conclusion that the safest weakness with which a woman can be afflicted is that romantic and ridiculous *faiblesse* called piety. So these two lived a happy life together, Berthe's share of it being very secluded, and were wonderfully little troubled by the turbulence with which society was making its tumultuous way to the virtuous serenity of republican perfection.

The communication announcing the project of the *ci-devant* Marquis for the secure exportation of his nephew, and containing the skilful appeal before mentioned, grievously disturbed the tranquillity of Prosper, and was precisely one of those incidents which he would especially have liked to conceal from his daughter. But he could not do so; the appeal was too cleverly made; and utter indifference to it, utter neglect of the letter, which naturally suggested itself as the easiest means of getting rid of a difficulty, would have involved an act of direct and uncompromising dishonesty to which Prosper,

though of sufficiently elastic conscience within the
limit of professional gains, could not contemplate.
The Château de Sénanges was indeed his own lawful property; his without prejudice to the former
owners, dispossessed by no act of his.   But the *ci-
devant* Marquis—confiding in him to an extent
which was quite astonishing, except on the *pis-aller*
theory, which is so unflattering as to be seldom accepted—announced to him the existence of a certain
packet, hidden in the château, acknowledging its
value, and urging the need of its safe transmission.
This was not his property.   He heartily wished he
had never learned its existence, but wishing that
was clearly of no use; then he wished the nephew
of the *ci-devant* might come soon, and take himself
and the hidden wealth away with all possible speed.
This latter was a more realizable desire, and Prosper settled his mind with it, communicated the interesting but decidedly dangerous secret to Berthe,
received her warm sanction, and transmitted to the
Marquis, by the appointed means, an assurance that
his wishes should be punctually carried out.   The
absence of an interdiction of his visit before a certain date was to be the signal to M. Paul de
Sénanges that he was to proceed to act upon his
uncle's instructions; he waited the proper time,
the reassuring silence was maintained unbroken,
and he ultimately set forth on his journey, and accomplished it in safety.

Preparations had been made at the Maison Alix
for the reception of M. Glaire, and his supposed
occupation had been announced.   The apartments
were decorated in a heavy, gloomy style, and those
of the *citoyenne* in particular (they had been occu-

pied by a lady who had once been designated as *feue Madame la Marquise,* but who was referred to now as *la mère du ci-devant*) were much in need of reno‧ vation. The alcove, for instance, was all that was least gay and most far from simple. The *citoyenne* would have all that changed. On the morning of the day of the expected arrival, Berthe said to her father:

"It would seem as if the Marquis did not know the exact spot in which the packet is deposited. M. Paul's assumed character implies the necessity for a search."

M. Henri Glaire arrived at the Maison Alix, was fraternally received, and made acquainted with the sphere of his operations. The young man had a good deal of both ability and taste in the line he had assumed, and the part was not difficult to play. Some days were judiciously allowed to pass before the real object of the masquerade was pursued, and during that time cordial relations established themselves between the *avocat* and his guest. The young man was handsome, elegant, engaging, with all the external advantages, and devoid of the vices, errors, and hopeless infatuated unscrupulousness, of his class; he had naturally quick intelligence, and some real knowledge and comprehension of life had been knocked into him by the hard-hitting blows of Fate. His face was like his mother's, Prosper Alix thought, and his mind and tastes were of the very pattern which, in theory, Berthe approved. Berthe, a very unconventional French girl—who thought the new era of purity, love, virtue, and disinterestedness ought to do away with marriage by barter as one of its most notable reforms, and

10

had been disenchanted by discovering that the
abolition of marriage altogether suited the taste of
the incorruptible Republic better—might like,
might even love, this young man. She saw so few
men, and had no fancy for patriots; she would certainly be obstinate about it if she did chance to love
him. This would be a nice state of affairs. This
would be a pleasant consequence of the confiding
request of the *ci-devant*. Prosper wished with all
his heart for the arrival of the concerted signal,
which should tell Henri Glaire that he might fulfil
the purpose of his sojourn at the Maison Alix, and
set forth for Marseilles.

But the signal did not come, and the days—long,
beautiful, sunny, soothing summer-days—went on.
The painting of the panels of the *citoyenne's* apartment, which she vacated for that purpose, pro-
gressed slowly; and M. Paul de Sénanges, guided
by the ground-plan, and aided by Berthe, had discovered the spot in which the jewels of price, almost
the last remnants of the princely wealth of the Sénanges, had been hidden by the *femme-de-chambre*
who had perished with her mistress, having con-
fided a general statement of the fact to a priest, for
transmission to the Marquis. This spot had been
ingeniously chosen. The sleeping-apartment of the
late Marquis was extensive, lofty, and provided
with an alcove of sufficiently large dimensions to
have formed in itself a handsome room. This
space, containing a splendid but gloomy bed, on an
estrade, and hung with rich faded brocade, was
divided from the general extent of the apartment
by a low railing of black oak, elaborately carved,
opening in the centre, and with a flat wide bar

along the top, covered with crimson velvet. The
curtains were contrived to hang from the ceiling,
and, when let down inside the screen of railing,
they matched the draperies which closed before the
great stone balcony at the opposite end of the room.
Since the *avocat's* daughter had occupied this pala-
tial chamber, the curtains of the alcove had never
been drawn, and she had substituted for them a
high folding screen of black-and-gold Japanese
pattern, also a relic of the grand old times, which
stood about six feet on the outside of the rails that
shut in her bed. The floor was of shining oak,
testifying to the conscientious and successful labors
of successive generations of *frotteurs;* and on the
spot where the railing of the alcove opened by a
pretty quaint device sundering the intertwined
arms of a pair of very chubby cherubs, a square
space in the floor was also richly carved.

The seekers soon reached the end of their search.
A little effort removed the square of carved oak,
and underneath they found a casket, evidently of
old workmanship, richly wrought in silver, much
tarnished but quite intact. It was agreed that this
precious deposit should be replaced, and the carved
square laid down over it, until the signal for his
departure should reach Paul. The little baggage
which under any circumstances he could have ventured to allow himself in the dangerous journey he
was to undertake, must be reduced, so as to admit
of his carrying the casket without exciting suspicion.

The finding of the hidden treasure was not the
first joint discovery made by the daughter of the *avocat* and the son of the *ci-devant*. The cogitations of
Prosper Alix were very wise, very reasonable; but

they were a little tardy. Before he had admitted
the possibility of mischief, the mischief was done.
Each had found out that the love of the other was
indispensable to the happiness of life; and they
had exchanged confidences, assurances, protesta-
tions, and promises, as freely, as fervently, and as
hopefully, as if no such thing as a Republic, one
and indivisible, with a keen scent and an unappeas-
able thirst for the blood of aristocrats, existed.
They forgot all about "Liberty, Fraternity, and
Equality"—these egotistical, narrow-minded young
people;—they also forgot the characteristic alternative to those unparalleled blessings—"Death."
But Prosper Alix did not forget any of these things;
and his consternation, his provision of suffering for
his beloved daughter, were terrible, when she told
him, with a simple noble frankness which the
grandes dames of the dead-and-gone time of great
ladies had rarely had a chance of exhibiting, that
she loved M. Paul de Sénanges, and intended to
marry him when the better times should come.
Perhaps she meant when that alternative of *death*
should be struck off the sacred formula;—of course
she meant to marry him with the sanction of her
father, which she made no doubt she should receive.

Prosper Alix was in pitiable perplexity. He
could not bear to terrify his daughter by a full explanation of the danger she was incurring; he could
not bear to delude her with false hope. If this
young man could be got away at once safely, there
was not much likelihood that he would ever be able
to return to France. Would Berthe pine for him,
or would she forget him, and make a rational, sensible, rich, republican marriage, which would not

imperil either her reputation for pure patriotism
or her father's? The latter would be the very best
thing that could possibly happen, and therefore it
was decidedly unwise to calculate upon it; but,
after all, it was possible; and Prosper had not the
courage, in such a strait, to resist the hopeful
promptings of a possibility. How ardently he re-
gretted that he had complied with the prayer of the
ci-devant! When would the signal for Mr. Paul's
departure come?

Prosper Alix had made many sacrifices, had
exercised much self-control for his daughter's sake;
but he had never sustained a more severe trial than
this, never suffered more than he did now, under
the strong necessity for hiding from her his absolute conviction of the impossibility of a happy result for this attachment, in that future to which
the lovers looked so fearlessly. He could not even
make his anxiety and apprehension known to Paul
de Sénanges; for he did not believe the young man
had sufficient strength of will to conceal anything
so important from the keen and determined observation of Berthe.

The expected signal was not given, and the lovers
were incautious. The seclusion of the Maison Alix
had all the danger, as well as all the delight, of
solitude, and Paul dropped his disguise too much
and too often. The servants, few in number, were
of the truest patriotic principles, and to some of
them the denunciation of the *citoyen*, whom they
condescended to serve because the sacred Revolution
had not yet made them as rich as he, would have
been a delightful duty, a sweet-smelling sacrifice
to be laid on the altar of the country. They heard

certain names and places mentioned; they perceived
many things which led them to believe that Henri
Glaire was not an industrial artist and pure patriot,
worthy of respect, but a wretched *ci-devant*, resort-
ing to the dignity of labor to make up for the right-
eous destruction of every other kind of dignity.
One day a gardener, of less stoical virtue than his
fellows, gave Prosper Alix a warning that the presence of a *ci-devant* upon his premises was suspected,
and that he might be certain a domiciliary visit, attended with dangerous results to himself, would
soon take place. Of course the *avocat* did not commit himself by any avowal to this lukewarm patriot;
but he casually mentioned that Henri Glaire was
about to take his leave. What was to be done?
He must not leave the neighborhood without receiving the instructions he was awaiting; but he
must leave the house, and be supposed to have
gone quite away. Without any delay or hesitation,
Prosper explained the facts to Berthe and her lover,
and insisted on the necessity for an instant parting. Then the courage and the readiness of the
girl told. There was no crying, and very little
trembling; she was strong and helpful.

"He must go to Pichon's, father," she said,
"and remain there until the signal is given.—
Pichon is a master-mason, Paul," she continued,
turning to her lover, "and his wife was my nurse.
They are avaricious people; but they are fond of
me in their way, and they will shelter you faith-
fully enough, when they know that my father will
pay them handsomely. You must go at once, unseen by the servants; they are at supper. Fetch
your valise, and bring it to my room, We will put

the casket in it, and such of your things as you must take out to make room for it, we can hide under the plank. My father will go with you to Pichon's, and we will communicate with you there as soon as it is safe."

Paul followed her to the large gloomy room where the treasure lay, and they took the casket from its hiding-place. It was heavy, though not large, and an awkward thing to pack away among linen in a small valise. They managed it, however, and, the brief preparation completed, the moment of parting arrived. Firmly and eloquently, though in haste, Berthe assured Paul of her changeless love and faith, and promised him to wait for him for any length of time in France, if better days should be slow of coming, or to join him in some foreign land, if they were never to come. Her father was present, full of compassion and misgiving. At length he said:

"Come, Paul, you must leave her; every moment is of importance."

The young man and his betrothed were standing on the spot whence they had taken the casket; the carved rail with the heavy curtains might have been the outer sanctuary of an altar, and they bride and bridegroom before it, with earnest, loving faces, and clasped hands.

"Farewell, Paul," said Berthe; "promise me once more, in this the moment of our parting, that you will come to me again, if you are alive, when the danger is past."

"Whether I am living or dead, Berthe," said Paul de Sénanges, strongly moved by some sudden inexplicable instinct, "I will come to you again."

In a few more minutes, Prosper Alix and his guest, who carried, not without difficulty, the small but heavy leather valise, had disappeared in the distance, and Berthe was on her knees before the *prie-dieu* of the *ci-devant* Marquise, her face turned toward the "Holy Hill" of Fourvières.

Pichon, *maître*, and his sons, *garçons-maçons*, were well-to-do people, rather morose, exceedingly avaricious, and of taciturn dispositions; but they were not ill spoken of by their neighbors. They had amassed a good deal of money in their time, and were just then engaged on a very lucrative job. This was the construction of several of the steep descents, by means of stairs, straight and winding, cut in the face of the *côteaux*, by which pedestrains are enabled to descend into the town. Pichon *père* was a *propriétaire* as well; his property was that which is now in the possession of Giraudier, *pharmacien, première classe*, and which was destined to attain a sinister celebrity during his proprietorship. One of the straightest and steepest of the stairways had been cut close to the *terre* which the mason owned, and a massive wall, destined to bound the high-road at the foot of the declivity, was in course of construction.

When Prosper Alix and Paul de Sénanges reached the abode of Pichon, the master-mason, with his sons and workmen, had just completed their day's work, and were preparing to eat the supper served by the wife and mother, a tall, gaunt woman, who looked as if a more liberal scale of housekeeping would have done her good, but on whose features the stamp of that devouring and degrading avarice which is the commonest vice of the French peasantry, was set as plainly as on the hard faces of her husband and her sons. The *avocat* explained his business and introduced his companion briefly, and awaited the reply of Pichon *père* without any appearance of inquietude.

"You don't run any risk," he said; "at least, you don't run any risk which I cannot make it worth your while to incur. It is not the first time you have received a temporary guest on my recommendation. You know nothing about the citizen Glaire, except that he is recommended to you by me. I am responsible; you can, on occasion, make me so. The citizen may remain with you a short time; can hardly remain long. Say, citizen, is it agreed? I have no time to spare."

It was agreed, and Prosper Alix departed, leaving M. Paul de Sénanges, convinced that the right, indeed the only, thing had been done, and yet much troubled and depressed.

Pichon *père* was a short, squat, powerfully built man, verging on sixty, whose thick, dark grizzled hair, sturdy limbs, and hard hands, on which the muscles showed like cords, spoke of endurance and strength; he was, indeed, noted in the neighborhood for those qualities. His sons resembled him slightly, and each other closely, as was natural, for they were twins. They were heavy, lumpish fellows, and they made but an ungracious return to the attempted civilities of the stranger, to whom the offer of their mother to show him his room was a decided relief. As he rose to follow the woman, Paul de Sénanges lifted his small valise with difficulty from the floor, on which he had placed it on entering the house, and carried it out of the room

in both his arms. The brothers followed these
movements with curiosity, and, when the door
closed behind their mother and the stranger, their
eyes met.

.   .   .   .   .   .

Twenty-four hours had passed away, and nothing new had occurred at the Maison Alix. The
servants had not expressed any curiosity respecting
the departure of the citizen Glaire, no domiciliary
visit had taken place, and Berthe and her father
were discussing the propriety of Prosper's ventur-
ing, on the pretext of an excursion in another direction, a visit to the isolated and quiet dwelling
of the master-mason. No signal had yet arrived.
It was agreed that after the lapse of another day,
if their tranquillity remained undisturbed, Prosper
Alix should visit Paul de Sénanges. Berthe, who
was silent and preoccupied, retired to her own room
early, and her father, who was uneasy and appre-
hensive, desperately anxious for the promised communication from the Marquis, was relieved by her
absence.

The moon was high in the dark sky, and her
beams were flung across the polished oak floor of
Berthe's bedroom, through the great window with
the stone balcony, when the girl, who had gone to
sleep with her lover's name upon her lips in prayer,
awoke with a sudden start, and sat up in her
bed. An unbearable dread was upon her; and
yet she was unable to utter a cry, she was unable
to make another movement. Had she heard a
voice? No, no one had spoken, nor did she fancy
that she heard any sound. But within her, some-

where inside her heaving bosom, something said,
"Berthe!"

And she listened, and knew what it was. And
it spoke, and said:

"I promised you that, living or dead, I would
come to you again. 'And I have come to you; but
not living."

She was quite awake. Even in the agony of her
fear she looked around, and tried to move her hands,
to feel her dress and the bedclothes, and to fix her
eyes on some familiar object, that she might satisfy
herself, before this racing and beating, this whirl-
ing and yet icy chilliness of her blood should kill
her outright, that she was really awake.

"I have come to you; but not living."

What an awful thing that voice speaking within
her was! She tried to raise her head and to look
toward the place where the moonbeams marked
bright lines upon the polished floor, which lost
themselves at the foot of the Japanese screen. She
forced herself to this effort, and lifted her eyes,
wild and haggard with fear, and there, the moonbeams at his feet, the tall black screen behind him,
she saw Paul de Sénanges. She saw him; she
looked at him quite steadily; she rose, slowly, with
a mechanical movement, and stood upright beside
her bed, clasping her forehead with her hands, and
gazing at him. He stood motionless, in the dress
he had worn when he took leave of her, the light-
colored riding-coat of the period, with a short cape,
and a large white cravat tucked into the double
breast. The white muslin was flecked, and the
front of the riding-coat was deeply stained, with
blood. He looked at her, and she took a step for-

ward—another—then, with a desperate effort, she dashed open the railing and flung herself on her knees before him, with her arms stretched out as if to clasp him. But he was no longer there; the moonbeams fell clear and cold upon the polished floor, and lost themselves where Berthe lay, at the foot of the screen, her head upon the ground, and every sign of life gone from her.

. . . .

"Where is the citizen Glaire?" asked Prosper Alix of the *citoyenne* Pichon, entering the house of the master-mason abruptly, and with a stern and threatening countenance. "I have a message for him; I must see him."

"I know nothing about him," replied the *citoyenne*, without turning in his direction, or relaxing her culinary labors. "He went away from here the next morning, and I did not trouble myself to ask where; that is his affair."

"He went away? Without letting me know! Be careful, *citoyenne*; this is a serious matter."

"So they tell me," said the woman with a grin, which was not altogether free from pain and fear; "for you! A serious thing to have a *suspect* in your house, and palm him off on honest people. However, he went away peaceably enough when he knew we had found him out, and that we had no desire to go to prison, or worse, on his account, or yours."

She was strangely insolent, this woman, and the listener felt his helplessness; he had brought the young man there with such secrecy, he had so carefully provided for the success of concealment.

"Who carried his valise?" Prosper Alix asked her suddenly.

"How should I know?" she replied; but her hands lost their steadiness, and she upset a stew-pan; "he carried it here, didn't he? and I suppose he.carried it away again."

Prosper Alix looked at her steadily—she shunned his gaze, but she showed no other sign of confusion; then horror and disgust of the woman came over him.

"I must see Pichon," he said; "where is he?"

"Where should he be but at the wall? he and the boys are working there, as always. The citizen can see them; but he will remember not to detain them; in a little quarter of an hour the soup will be ready."

The citizen did see the master-mason and his sons, and after an interview of some duration he left the place in a state of violent agitation and complete discomfiture. The master-mason had addressed to him these words at parting:

"I assert that the man went away at his own free will; but if you do not keep very quiet, I shall deny that he came here at all—you cannot prove he did—and I will denounce you for harboring a *suspect* and *ci-devant* under a false name. I know a De Sénanges when I see him as well as you, citizen Alix; and, wishing M. Paul a good journey, I hope you will consider about this matter, for truly, my friend, I think you will sneeze in the sack before I shall."

.   .   .   .   .   .

"We must bear it, Berthe, my child," said Prosper Alix to his daughter many weeks later, when the fever had left her, and she was able to talk with her father of the mysterious and frightful events which had occurred. "We are utterly help-less. There is no proof, only the word of these wretches against mine, and certain destruction to me if I speak. We will go to Spain, and tell the Marquis all the truth, and never return, if you would rather not. But, for the rest, we must bear it."

"Yes, my father," said Berthe submissively, "I know we must; but God need not, and I don't be-lieve He will."

The father and the daughter left France un-molested, and Berthe "bore it" as well as she could. When better times come they returned, Prosper Alix an old man, and Berthe a stern, silent, hand-some woman, with whom no one associated any notions of love or marriage. But long before their return the traditions of the Croix Rousse were en-riched by circumstances which led to that before-mentioned capital bargain made by the father of the Giraudier of the present. These circumstances were the violent death of Pichon and his two sons, who were killed by the fall of a portion of the great boundary-wall on the very day of its completion, and the discovery, close to its foundation, at the extremity of Pichon's *terre*, of the corpse of a young man attired in a light-colored riding-coat, who had been stabbed through the heart.

Berthe Alix lived alone in the Château de Sénan-ges, under its restored name, until she was a very old woman. She lived long enough to see the golden figure on the summit of the "Holy Hill," long enough to forget the bad old times, but not long enough to forget or cease to mourn the lover who had kept his promise, and come back to her; the lover who rested in the earth which once covered the bones of the martyrs, and who kept a place for her by his side. She has filled that place for many years. You may see it, when you look down from the second gallery of the bell-tower at Fourvières, following the bend of the outstretched golden arm of Notre Dame.

The château was pulled down some years ago, and there is no trace of its former existence among the vines.

Good times, and bad times, and again good times have come for the Croix Rousse, for Lyons, and for France, since then; but the remembrance of the treachery of Pichon & Sons, and of the retribution which at once exposed and punished their crime, outlives all changes. And once, every year, on a certain summer night, three ghostly figures are seen, by any who have courage and patience to watch for them, gliding along by the foot of the boundary-wall, two of them carrying a dangling corpse, and the other, implements for mason's work and a small leather valise. Giraudier, *pharmacien*, has never seen these ghostly figures, but he describes them with much minuteness; and only the *esprits forts* of the Croix Rousse deny that the ghosts of Pichon & Sons are not yet laid.

THE PHANTOM FOURTH.

11

THE PHANTOM FOURTH.

THEY were three.
It was in the cheap night-service train from Paris to Calais that I first met them.

Railways, as a rule, are among the many things which they do *not* order better in France, and the French Northern line is one of the worst managed in the world, barring none, not even the Italian *vie ferrate.* I make it a rule, therefore, to punish the directors of, and the shareholders in, that undertaking to the utmost within my limited ability, by spending as little money on their line as I can help.

It was, then, in a third-class compartment of the train that I met the three.

Three as hearty, jolly-looking Saxon faces, with stalwart frames to match, as one would be likely to meet in an hour's walk from the Regent's Park to the Mansion House.

One of the three was dark, the other two were fair. The dark one was the senior of the party. He wore an incipient full beard, evidently in process of training, with a considerable amount of grizzle in it.

The face of one of his companions was graced with a magnificent flowing beard. The third of the party, a fair-haired youth of some twenty-three

163

or four summers, showed a scrupulously smooth-shaven face.

They looked all three much flushed and slightly excited, and, I must say, they turned out the most boisterous set of fellows I ever met.

They were clearly gentlemen, however, and men of education, with considerable linguistic acquire-ments; for they chatted and sang, and declaimed and "did orations" all the way from Paris to Calais, in a slightly bewildering variety of tongues.

Their jollity had, perhaps, just a little over-tinge of the slap-bang jolly-dog style in it; but there was so much heartiness and good-nature in all they said and in all they did, that it was quite impossible for any of the other occupants of the carriage to vote them a nuisance; and even the sourest of the officials, whom they chaffed most unmercifully and unremittingly at every station on the line, took their punishment with a shrug and a grin. The only person, indeed, who rose against them in indignant protestation was the head-waiter at the Calais station refreshment-room, to whom they would persist in propounding puzzling prob-lems, such as, for instance, "If you charge two shillings for one-and-a-half-ounce slice of breast of veal, how many fools will it take to buy the joint of you?"—and what *he* got by the attempt to stop their chaff was a caution to any other sinner who might have felt similarly inclined.

As for me, I could only give ·half my sense of hearing to their utterings, the other half being put under strict sequester at the time by my friend O'Kweene, the great Irish philosopher, who was delivering to me, for my own special behoof and benefit, a brilliant, albeit somewhat abstruse, dissertation on the "visible and palpable outward manifestations of the inner consciousness of the soul in a trance;" which occupied all the time from Paris to Calais, full eight hours, and which, to judge from my feelings at the time, would certainly afford matter for three heavy volumes of reading in bed, in cases of inveterate sleeplessness— a hint to enterprising publishers.

My friend O'Kweene, who intended to stay a few days at Calais, took leave of me on the pier, and I went on board the steamer that was to carry us and the mail over to Dover.

Here I found our trio of the railway-car, snugly ensconced under an extemporized awning, artfully constructed with railway-rugs and greatcoats, supported partly against the luggage, and partly upon several oars, purloined from the boats, and turned into tent-poles for the nonce—which made the skipper swear wofully when he found it out some time after.

The three were even more cheery and boisterous on board than they had been on shore. From what I could make out in the dark, they were discussing the contents of divers bottles of liquor; I counted four dead men dropped quietly overboard by them in the course of the hour and a half we had to wait for the arrival of the mail-train, which was late, as usual on this line.

At last we were off, about half-past two o'clock in the morning. It was a beautiful, clear, moonlit night, so clear, indeed, that we could see the Dover lights almost from Calais harbor. But we had considerably more than a capful of wind, and there

was a turgent ground-swell on, which made our
boat—double-engined, and as trim and tidy a craft
as ever sped across the span from shore to shore—
behave rather lively, with sportive indulgence in a
brisk game of pitch-and-toss that proved anything
but comfortable to most of the passengers.

When we were steaming out of Calais harbor,
our three friends, emerging from beneath their
tent, struck up in chorus Campbell's noble song,
"Ye Mariners of England," finishing up with a
stave from "Rule, Britannia!"

But, alas for them! however loudly their throats
were shouting forth the sway proverbially held by
Albion and her sons over the waves, on this occasion at least the said waves seemed determined
upon ruling these particular three Britons with a
rod of antimony; for barely a few seconds after
the last vibrating echoes of the "Britons never,
never, never shall be slaves!" had died away upon
the wind, I beheld the three leaning lovingly together, in fast friendship linked, over the rail,
conversing in deep ventriguttural accents with the
denizens of Neptune's watery realm.

We had one of the quickest passages on record—
ninety-three minutes' steaming carried us across
from shore to shore. When we were just on the
point of landing, I heard the dark senior of the
party mutter to his companions, in a hollow whis-
per and mysterious manner, "He is gone again;"
to which the others, the bearded and the smooth-
shaven, responded in the same way, with deep sighs
of evident relief, "Ay, marry! so he is at last."

This mysterious communication roused my curiosity. Who was the party that was said to be

gone at last? Where had he come from? where had he been hiding, that *I* had not seen him? and where was he gone to now? I determined to know; if but the opportunity would offer, to screw, by cunning questioning, the secret out of either of the three.

Fate favored my design.

For some inscrutable reason, known only to the company's officials, we cheap-trainers were not permitted to proceed on our journey to London along with the mail, but were left to kick our heels for some two hours at the Dover station.

I went into the refreshment-room to look for my party; I had a notion I should find them where the Briton's unswerving and unerring instinct would be most likely to lead them. It turned out that I was right in my conjecture. There they were, seated round a table with huge bowls of steaming tea and monster piles of buttered toast and muffins spread on the festive board before them. Ay, indeed, there they were; but *quantum mutati ab illis!* how strangely changed from the noisy, rollicking set I had known them in the railway-car and on board the steamer, ere yet the demon of sea-sickness had claimed them for his own! How ghastly sober they looked now, to be sure! And how sternly and silently bent upon devoting themselves to the swilling of the Chinese shrub infusion and to the gorging of indigestible muffins. It was quite clear to me that it would have been worse than folly to venture upon addressing them while thus absorbed in absorbing. So I resolved to await a more favorable opening, and went out meanwhile to walk on the platform.

A short time I was left in solitary possession of the promenade; then I became suddenly aware that another traveller was treading the same ground with me—it was the dark elderly leader of the three. I glanced at him as he passed me under one of the lamps. He looked pale and sad. The furrowed lines on his brow bespoke deliberation deep and pondering profound. All the infinite mirth of the preceding few hours had departed from him, leaving him but a wretched wreck of his former reckless self.

"A fine night, sir," I said to break the ice—"for the season of the year," I added by way of a saving clause, to tone down the absoluteness of the assertion.

He looked at me abstractedly, merely reëchoing my own words, "A fine night, sir, for the season of the year."

"Why look ye so sad now, who were erst so jolly?" I bluntly asked, determined to force him into conversation.

"Ay, indeed, why so sad now?" he replied, looking me full in the face; then, suddenly clasping my arm with a spasmodic grip, he continued hurriedly, "I think I had best confide our secret to you. You seem a man of thought. I witnessed and admired the patient attention with which you listened to your friend's abstruse talk in the railway-car. Maybe you can find the solution of a mystery which defies the ponderings of our poor brains—mine and my two friends."

Then he proceeded to pour into my attentive ear this gruesome tale of mystery:

"We three—that is, myself, yon tall bearded

Briton," pointing to the glass door of the refreshment-room, "whose name is Jack Hobson, and
young Emmanuel Topp, junior partner in a great
beer firm, whom you may behold now at his fifth
bowl of tea and his seventh muffin—are teetotallers——"

"Teetotallers!" I could not help exclaiming.
"Lord bless me! that is certainly about the last
thing I should have taken you for, either of you."

"Well," he replied with some slight confusion,
"at least, we *were total* teetotallers, though I admit
we can now only claim the character of partial
abstainers. The fact is, when, about a fortnight
ago, we were discussing the plan of our projected
visit to the great Paris Exhibition, Topp suggested
that while in France we should do as the French
do, to which Jack Hobson assented, remarking
that the French knew nothing about tea, and that
a Frenchman's tea would be sure to prove an Eng-
lishman's poison. So we resolved to suspend the
pledge during our visit to France.

"It was on the second day after our arrival in
Paris. We were dining in a private cabinet at
Désiré Beaurain's, one of the leading restaurants
on the fashionable side of the Montmartre—Italiens
Boulevard. Our dinner was what an Irishman
might call a most 'illigant' affair. We had sipped
several bottles of Sauterne, and tasted a few of
Tavel, and we were just topping the entertainment
with a solitary bottle of champagne, when I became
suddenly aware of the presence of another party in
the room—a *fourth man*—who sat him down at our
table, and helped himself liberally to our liquor.
From what I ascertained afterward from Jack

Hobson and Emmanuel Topp, the intruder's presence became revealed to them also, either about the same time or a little later. What was he like? I cannot tell. His figure and face remained indistinct throughout—phantom-like. His features seemed endowed with a stronge weird mobility that would defyingly elude the fixing grasp of our eager eyes. Now, and to my two companions, he would look marvellously like me; then, to me, he would stalk and rave about in the likeness of Jack Hobson; again, he would seem the counterfeit of Emmanuel Topp; then he would look like all the three of us put together; then like neither of us, nor like anybody else. Oh, sir, it was a woful thing to be haunted by this phantom apparition. Yet the strangest part of the affair was that neither of us seemed to feel a whit surprised at the dread presence; that we quietly and uncomplainingly let him drink our wine, and actually give orders for more; that we never objected, in fact, to any of his sayings and doings. What seemed also strange was that the waiter, while yet receiving and executing his orders, was evidently pretending to ignore his presence. But then, as I dare say you know as well as I do, French waiters are *such* actors!

" Well, to resume, there he was, this fourth man, seated at our table and feasting at our expense. And the pranks that he would play us — they were truly stupendous. He began his little game by ordering in half-a-dozen of champagne. And when the waiter seemed slightly doubtful and hesitating about executing the order, Topp, forsooth, must put in his oar, and indorse the command, actually pretending that *I,* who am now

speaking to you, and who am the very last man in
the world likely to dream of such a preposterous
thing, had given the order, and that I was a jolly
old brick, and the best of boon companions. Surprise at this barefaced assertion kept me mute, and
so, of course, the champagne was brought in, and
I thought the best thing to do under the circumstances was to have my share of it at least; and so
I had—my fair share; but, bless you, it was nothing to what that fourth man drank of it. In fact,
the amount of liquor *he* would swill on this and on
the many subsequent occasions he intruded his
presence upon us, was a caution.

"We paid our little bill without grumbling,
though the presence of the fourth man at our table
had added rather heavily to the *addition*, as they
call bills at French restaurants.

"We sallied forth into the street to get a whiff
of fresh air. *He*, the demon, pertinaciously stuck
to us; he familiarly linked his arm through mine,
and, suggesting coffee as rather a good thing to take
after dinner, took us over to the Café du Cardinal,
where he, however, took none of the Arabian bev-
erage himself (there being only three cups placed
for us, as I distinctly saw), but drank an intermin-
able succession of *chasse-café*, utterly regardless of
the divisional lines of the cognac *carafon*. Part
of these he would take neat, another portion he
would burn over sugar, gloating glaringly over the
bluish flame, while gleams of demoniac delight
would flit across his ever-changing features. Jack
Hobson and Topp, I am sorry to say, joined him
with a will in this double-distilled debauch; and
when I attempted to remonstrate with them, they

brazenly asserted that *I*, who am now speaking to
you, who have always, publicly and privately, declared brandy to be the worst of evil spirits, had
taken more of it, to my own cheek, as they slang-
ily expressed it, than the two of them together;
and the waiter, who had evidently been bribed by
them, boldly maintained that *le vieux monsieur*, as
he had the impudence to call me, had swallowed
plus de trois carafons de fine; whereupon the
fourth man, stepping up to him, punched his head,
which served him right. Now you will hardly believe me when I tell you that at that very instant
Topp forced me back into my chair, while Jack
Hobson pinioned my arms from behind, and the
waiter had the unblushing effrontery to stamp and
rave at me like a maniac, demanding satisfaction
or compensation at my hands for the unprovoked
assault committed upon him by *me, coram populo!*
—by *me*, who, I beg to assure you, am the most
peaceable man living, and am actually famed for
the mildness of my disposition and the sweetness
and suavity of my temper. And, would you believe it? everybody present, waiters and guests,
and my own two bosom-friends, joined in the con-
spiracy against me, and I actually had to give the
wretch of a waiter ten francs as a plaster for his
broken pate, and a salve for his wounded honor!
Where was the real culprit all this time, you ask
me—the fourth man? Why, he quietly stood by
grinning, and they all and every one of them pretended not to see him, though Topp and Jack
Hobson next morning confessed to me that they
certainly had an indistinct consciousness of the
presence throughout of this miserable intruder.

"How we finished that night I remember not; nor could Jack Hobson or Emmanuel Topp. All we could conscientiously stand by, if we were questioned, is that we awoke next morning—the three of us—with some slight swimming in our heads, and a hazy recollection of a gorgeous dream of brilliant lights and sounds of music and revelry, and bright visions of groves and grottoes, and dancing houris (or hussies, as moral Jack Hobson calls the poor things), and a hot supper at a certain place in the Passage des Princes, of which I think the name is Peter's.

"I will not tire your courteous patience by a detailed narrative of our experiences day after day, during our fortnight's stay in Paris. Suffice it to tell you that from that time forward to yesterday, when we left, the *fourth man,* as we, by mutual consent, agreed to call the phantom apparition, came in regularly to our dinner; with the dessert or a little after; that he would constantly suggest a fresh supply of Côte St. Jacques, Moulin-à-Vent, Beaune, Chambertin, Roederer Carte Blanche, and a variety of other, generally rather more than less expensive, wines—and that he somehow would manage to make us have them, too.

"Then he would sally forth with us to the café, where he would indulge in irritating chaff of the waiters, and in slighting comments upon the great French nation in general, and the Parisians in particular, and upon their institutions and manners and customs.

"He would insist upon singing the Marseillaise; he would speak disparagingly of the Emperor, whom he would irreverently call Lambert; he would pass cutting and unsavory remarks upon the glorious system of the night-carts; he would call down the judgment of Heaven upon the devoted head of poor Mr. Haussmann; he would go up to some unhappy sergent-de-ville, who might, however unwittingly, excite his ire, and tell him a bit of his mind in English, with sarcastic allusions to his cocket-hat and his toasting-fork, and polite inquiries after the health of *ce cher* Monsieur Lambert, or the whereabouts of *cet excellent* Monsieur Godinot. The worst of the matter was that I suppose for the reason that man is an imitative animal, a sort of πίθηκος μύωρος, or Monboddian monkey minus the tail—my two companions were, somehow, always sure to join the wretch in his evil behavior, and to go on just as bad as he did. No wonder, then, that we got into no end of rows, and it is a marvel to me now, how ever we have managed to get off with a whole skin to our bodies.

"He would insist upon taking us to Mabille, the Closerie des Lilas, and the Châteaurouge, where he would indulge in the maddest pranks and antics, and somehow lead us to join in the wildest dances, and make us lift our legs as high as the highest lifter among the *habitués*, male or female.

"One night, at about half-past two in the morning (*Hibernicè*), he had the cool assurance to drag us along with him to the then closed entrance to the Passage des Princes, where he frantically shook the gate, and insisted to the frightened concierge, who came running up in his night-shirt, that Peter's must and ought to be open still, as *we* had not had our supper yet; and Topp and Jack Hobson, forsooth, must join in the row.

I have no distinct recollection of whether it was our phantom guest or either of my companions that madly strove to detain the hastily retreating form of the concierge by a desperate clutch at the tail of his shirt; I only remember that the garment gave way in the struggle, and that the unhappy functionary was reduced nearly altogether to the primitive buff costume of the father of man in Paradise ere he had put his teeth into that unlucky apple of which, the pips keep so inconveniently sticking in poor humanity's gizzard to the present day. And what I remember also to my cost is, that the sergent-de-ville, whom the bereaved man's shouts of distress brought to the scene, fastened upon *me*, the most inoffensive of mortals, for a compensation fine of twenty francs, as if *I* had been the culprit. And deuced glad we were, I assure you, to get off without more serious damage to our pocket and reputation than this, and a copious volley of *sacrés ivrognes Anglais*, fired at us by the wretched concierge and his friend of the police, who, I am quite sure, went halves with him in the compensation. Ah! they are a lawless set, these French.

"On another occasion we three went to the Exhibition, where we visited one of our colonial departments, in company with several English friends, and some French gentlemen appointed on the wine jury. We went to taste a few samples of colonial wines. *He* was not with us *then*. Barely, however, had we uncorked a poor dozen bottles, which turned out rather good for colonial, though a little raw and slightly uneducated, when *who* should stalk in but our fourth man, as jaunty and unconcerned as ever. Well, *he* fell to tasting, and he soon grew eloquent in praise of the colonial juice, which he declared would, in another twenty years' time, be fit to compete successfully with the best French vintages. Of course, the French gentlemen with us could not stand *this;* they spoke slightingly of the British colonial, and one of them even went so far as to call it rotgut. I cannot say whether it was the spirit of the uncompromising opinion thus pronounced, or the coarsely indelicate way in which the judgment of our French friend was expressed, that riled our phantom guest— enough, it brought him down in full force upon the offender and his countrymen, with most fluent French vituperation and an unconscionable amount of bad jokes and worse puns, finishing up with a general address to them as members of the *disgusting* jury, instead of jury of *dégustation.* Now, this I should not have minded so much; for, I must confess, I felt rather nettled at the national conceit and prejudice of these French. But the wretch, in the impetuous utterance of his invective, must somehow—though I was not aware of it at the time—have mimicked my gestures and imitated the very tones and accent of my voice so closely as to deceive even some of my English companions: or how else to account for the fact of their calling me a noisy brawler and a pestilent nuisance? *me,* the gentlest and mildest-spoken of mortals!

"Before our departure from London we had calculated our probable expenses on a most liberal scale, and we had made comfortable provision accordingly for a few weeks' stay in Paris. But with the additional heavy burden of the franking of so copious an imbiber as our fourth man thus unexpectedly thrown on our shoulders, it was no great wonder that we should find our resources go much faster than we had anticipated; so we had already been forcedly. led to bethink ourselves of shortening our intended stay in the French capital when a fresh exploit of the phantom fourth, climaxing all his past misdeeds, brought matters to a crisis.

"It was the day before yesterday, the 4th of September. We had been dining at Marigny, and dancing at Mabille. Our eccentric guest had come in, as usual, with the champagne, and had of course, after dinner, taken us over to the enchanted gardens. We were all very jolly. *He* suggested supper at the Cascades, in the Bois de Boulogne. We chartered a *fiacre* to take us there and back. We supped rather copiously. *He* somehow made our coachman drunk, and took upon himself to drive us home. Need I tell you that he upset us in the Avenue de l'Impératrice, and that we had to walk it, and pretty fast too? It was a mercy there were no bones broken.

"Well, as we were walking along, just barely recovering from the shock of the accident, he suddenly·took some new whim into his confounded noddle. Nothing would do for him but he must drag us along with him to the great entrance of the Elysée Napoléon (which erst was, and maybe is soon likely to be once more, the Elysée Bourbon), where he had the brazen impudence to claim admittance, as the Emperor, he pretended, had been graciously pleased to offer us the splendid hospitality of that renowned mansion. What

12

further happened here, neither I nor either of my friends can tell. Our recollections from this period till next morning are doubtful and indistinct. All we can state for certain is, that yesterday morning we awoke, the three of us, in a most wretched state, in a strange, nasty place. We learn soon after from a gentleman in a cocked hat, who came to visit us on business, that the imperial hospitality which we had claimed last night had indeed been extended to us—only in the *violon*, instead of the Elysée. Our phantom guest was gone: he would alway, somehow sneak away in the morning, when there was nothing left for him to drink—the guzzling villain!

"The gentleman in the cocked-hat pressingly invited us to pay a visit to the Commissaire du Quartier. That formidable functionary received us with the customary French-polished veneer of urbanity which, as a rule, constitutes the *suaviter in modo* of the higher class of Gallic officials. He read us a severe lecture, however, upon the alleged impropriety of our conduct; and when I ventured to protest that it was not to us the blame ought to be imputed, but to the *quatrième*, he mistook my meaning, and, ere I could explain myself, he cut me short with a polite remark that the French used the cardinal instead of the ordinal numbers in stating the days of the month, with the exception of the first, and that he had had too much trouble with our countrymen (he took us for Yankees!) on the 4th of July, to be disposed to look with an over-lenient eye upon the vagaries we had chosen to commit on the 4th of September, which he supposed was another great national day with us. He

would, however, let us off this time with a simple
reprimand, upon payment of one hundred francs,
compensation for damage done to the coach—
drunken cabby having turned up, of course, to
testify against us. Well, we paid the money, and
handed the worthy magistrate twenty francs
besides, for the benefit of the poor, by way of acknowledgment for the imperial hospitality we had
enjoyed. We were then allowed to depart in peace.

"Now, you'll hardly believe it, I dare say, but
it is the truth notwithstanding, that we three, who
have been fast friends for years, actually began to
quarrel among ourselves now, mutually imputing
to one another the blame of all our misadventures
and misfortunes since our arrival in Paris, while
yet we clearly knew and felt, each and every of
us, that it was all the doings of that phantom
fourth.

"One thing, however, we all agreed to do—to
leave Paris by the first train.

"To fortify ourselves for the coming journey,
we went to indulge in the luxury of a farewell
breakfast at Désiré Beaurain's. Of course we
emptied a few bottles to our reconciliation. I do
not exactly remember how many, but this I *do*
remember, that our irrepressible incubus walked in
again, and took his place in the midst of us rather
sooner even than he had been wont to do; and he
never left us from that time to the moment of our
landing at Dover harbor, when he took his, I hope
and trust final, departure with a ghastly grin.

"I dare say you must have thought us a most
noisy and obstreperous lot: well, with my hand
on my heart, I can assure you, on my conscience,

that a quieter and milder set of fellows than us
three you are not likely to find on this or the other
side the Channel. But for that mysterious phantom fourth——"

Here the whistle sounded, and the guard came
up to us with a hurried, "Now then, gents, take
your seats, please; train is off in half a minnit!"

"What can have become of Topp and Jack Hobson?" muttered my new friend, looking around
him with eager scrutiny. "I should not wonder
if they were still refreshing." And he started off
in the direction of the refreshment-room.

I took my seat. Immediately after the train
whirled off. I cannot say whether the three were
left behind; all I know is that I did not see them
get out at London Bridge.

Remembering, however, that the appalling secret
of the supernatural visitation which had thus
harassed my three fellow-travellers had been con-
fided to me under the impression that I might be
likely to find a solution of the mystery, I have ever
since deeply pondered thereon.

Shallow thinkers, and sneerers uncharitably
given, may, from a consideration of the times,
places, and circumstances at and under which the
abnormal phenomena here recited were stated to
have been observed, be led to attribute them simply
to the promptings and imaginings of brains over-
heated by excessive indulgence in spirituous liquors.
But I, striving to be mindful always of the great
scriptural injunction to judge not, lest we be
judged, and opportunely remembering my friend
O'Kweene's learned dissertation above alluded to,
feel disposed to pronounce the apparition of the

phantom of the fourth man, and all the sayings, doings, and demeanings of the same, to have been simply so many visible and palpable outward manifestations of the inner consciousness of the souls of the three, and more notably of that of the elderly senior of the party, in a succession of vino-alcoholic trances.

My friend O'Kweene is, of course, welcome to such credit as may attach to this attempted solution of mine.

THE SPIRIT'S WHISPER.

THE SPIRIT'S WHISPER.

YES, I have been haunted!—haunted so fearfully that for some little time I thought myself insane. I was no raving maniac; I mixed in society as heretofore, although perhaps a trifle more grave and taciturn than usual; I pursued my daily avocations; I employed myself even on literary work. To all appearance I was one of the sanest of the sane; and yet all the while I considered myself the victim of such strange delusions that, in my own mind, I fancied my senses—and one sense in particular—so far erratic and beyond my own control that I was, in real truth, a mad-man. How far I was then insane it must be for others, who hear my story, to decide. My hallucinations have long since left me, and, at all events, I am now as sane as I suppose most men are.

My first attack came on one afternoon when, being in a listless and an idle mood, I had risen from my work and was amusing myself with speculating at my window on the different personages who were passing before me. At that time I occupied apartments in the Brompton Road. Perhaps, there is no thoroughfare in London where the ordinary passengers are of so varied a description or high life and low life mingle in so perpetual a medley. South-Kensington carriages there jostle costermongers' carts; the clerk in the public office, returning to his suburban dwelling, brushes the laborer coming from his work on the never-ending modern constructions in the new district; and the ladies of some of the surrounding squares flaunt the most gigantic of *chignons*, and the most exuberant of motley dresses, before the envying eyes of the ragged girls with their vegetable-baskets.

There was, as usual, plenty of material for observation and conjecture in the passengers, and their characters or destinations, from my window on that day. Yet I was not in the right cue for the thorough enjoyment of my favorite amusement. I was in a rather melancholy mood. Somehow or other, I don't know why, my memory had reverted to a pretty woman whom I had not seen for many years. She had been my first love, and I had loved her with a boyish passion as genuine as it was intense. I thought my heart would have broken, and I certainly talked seriously of dying, when she formed an attachment to an ill-conditioned, handsome young adventurer, and, on her family objecting to such an alliance, eloped with him. I had never seen the fellow, against whom, however, I cherished a hatred almost as intense as my passion for the infatuated girl who had flown from her home for his sake. We had heard of her being on the Continent with her husband, and learned that the man's shifty life had eventually taken him to the East. For some years nothing more had been heard of the poor girl. It was a melancholy history, and its memory ill-disposed me for amusement.

A sigh was probably just escaping my lips with the half-articulated words, "Poor Julia!" when my eyes fell on a man passing before my window. There was nothing particularly striking about him. He was tall, with fine features, and a long, fair beard, contrasting somewhat with his bronzed complexion. I had seen many of our officers on their return from the Crimea look much the same. Still, the man's aspect gave me a shuddering feeling, I didn't know why. At the same moment, a whispering, low voice uttered aloud in my ear the words, "It is he!" I turned, startled; there was no one near me, no one in the room. There was no fancy in the sound; I had heard the words with painful distinctness. I ran to the door, opened it—not a sound on the staircase, not a sound in the whole house—nothing but the hum from the street. I came back and sat down. It was no use reasoning with myself; I had the ineffaceable conviction that I had heard the voice. Then first the idea crossed my mind that I might be the victim of hallucinations. Yes, it must have been so, for now I recalled to mind that the voice had been that of my poor lost Julia; and at the moment I heard it I had been dreaming of her. I questioned my own state of health. I was well; at least I had been so, I felt fully assured, up to that moment. Now a feeling of chilliness and numbness and faintness had crept over me, a cold sweat was on my forehead. I tried to shake off this feeling by bringing back my thoughts to some other subject. But, involuntarily as it were, I again uttered the words, "Poor Julia!" aloud. At the same time a deep and heavy sigh, almost a groan, was distinctly audible close by me. I sprang up; I was alone—quite alone. It was, once more, an hallucination.

By degrees the first painful impression wore
away. Some days had passed, and I had begun to
forget my singular delusion. When my thoughts
did revert to it, the recollection was dismissed as
that of a ridiculous fancy. One afternoon I was
in the Strand, coming from Charing Cross, when I
was once more overcome by that peculiar feeling of
cold and numbness which I had before experienced.
The day was warm and bright and genial, and yet
I positively shivered. I had scarce time to interro-
gate my own strange sensations when a man went
by me rapidly. How was it that I recognized him
at once as the individual who had only passed my
window so casually on that morning of the hallucination? I don't know, and yet I was aware that
this man was the tall, fair passer-by of the Brompton Road. At the same moment the voice I had
previously heard whispered distinctly in my ear
the words, "Follow him!" I stood stupefied. The
usual throngs of indifferent persons were hurrying
past me in that crowded thoroughfare, but I felt
convinced that not one of these had spoken to me.
I remained transfixed for a moment. I was bent on
a matter of business in the contrary direction to the
individual I had remarked, and so, although with
unsteady step, I endeavored to proceed on my way.
Again that voice said, still more emphatically, in
my ear, "Follow him!" I stopped involuntarily.
And a third time, "Follow him!" I told myself
that the sound was a delusion, a cheat of my senses,
and yet I could not resist the spell. I turned to
follow. Quickening my pace, I soon came up with
the tall, fair man, and, unremarked by him, I followed him. Whither was this foolish pursuit to

lead me? It was useless to ask myself the question—I was impelled to follow.

I was not destined to go very far, however. Before long the object of my absurd chase entered a well-known insurance-office. I stopped at the door of the establishment: I had no business within, why should I continue to follow? Had I not already been making a sad fool of myself by my ridiculous conduct? These were my thoughts as I stood heated by my quick walk. Yes, heated; and yet, once more, came the sudden chill. Once more that same low but now awful voice spoke in my ear: "Go in!" it said. I endeavored to resist the spell, and yet I felt that resistance was in vain. Fortunately, as it seemed to me, the thought crossed my mind that an old acquaintance was a clerk in that same insurance-office. I had not seen the fellow for a great length of time, and I never had been very intimate with him. But here was a pretext; and so I went in and inquired for Clement Stanley. My acquaintance came forward. He was very busy, he said. I invented, on the spur of the moment, some excuse of the most frivolous and absurd nature, as far as I can recollect, for my intrusion.

"By the way," I said, as I turned to take my leave, although my question was "by the way" of nothing at all, "who was that tall, fair man who just now entered the office?"

"Oh, that fellow?" was the indifferent reply; "a Captain Campbell, or Canton, or some such name; I forget what. He is gone in before the board— insured his wife's life—and she is dead; comes for a settlement, I suppose."

There was nothing more to be gained, and so I

left the office. As soon as I came without into the
scorching sunlight, again the same feeling of cold,
again the same voice—" Wait!" Was I going mad?
More and more the conviction forced itself upon
me that I was decidedly a monomaniac already. I
felt my pulse. It was agitated and yet not fever-
ish. I was determined not to give way to this absurd hallucination; and yet, so far was I out of my
senses, that my will was no longer my own. Resolved as I was to go, I listened to the dictates of
that voice and waited. What was it to me that
this Campbell or Canton had insured his wife's life,
that she was dead, and that he wanted a settlement
of his claim? Obviously nothing; and I yet
waited.

So strong was the spell on me that I had no
longer any count of time. I had no consciousness
whether the period was long or short that I stood
there near the door, heedless of all the throng that
passed, gazing on vacancy. The fiercest of policemen might have told me to " move on," and I should
not have stirred, spite of all the terrors of the " station." The individual came forth. He paid no
heed to me. Why should he? What was I to
him? This time I needed no warning voice to bid
me follow. I was a madman, and I could not resist the impulses of my madness. It was thus, at
least I reasoned with myself. I followed into Regent Street. The object of my insensate observation lingered, and looked around as if in expectation. Presently a fine-looking woman, somewhat
extravagantly dressed, and obviously not a lady,
advanced toward him on the pavement. At the
sight of her he quickened his step, and joined her

rapidly. I shuddered again, but this time a sort
of dread was mingled with that strange shivering.
I knew what was coming, and it came. Again
that voice in my ear. "Look and remember!" it
said. I passed the man and woman as they stopped
at their first meeting.

"Is all right, George?" said the female.

"All right, my girl," was the reply.

I looked. An evil smile, as if of wicked triumph,
was on the the man's face, I thought. And on the
woman's? I looked at her, and I remembered. I
could not be mistaken. Spite of her change in
manner, dress, and appearance, it was Mary
Simms. This woman some years before, when she
was still very young, had been a sort of humble
companion to my mother. A simple-minded, honest girl, we thought her. Sometimes I had fancied
that she had paid me, in a sly way, a marked attention. I had been foolish enough to be flattered
by her stealthy glances and her sighs. But I had
treated these little demonstrations of partiality as
due only to a silly girlish fancy. Mary Simms,
however, had come to grief in our household. She
had been detected in the abstraction of sundry
jewels and petty ornaments. The morning after
discovery she had left the house, and we had heard
of her no more. As these recollections passed
rapidly through my mind I looked behind me.
The couple had turned back. I turned to follow
again; and spite of carriages and cabs, and shouts
and oaths of drivers, I took the middle of the street
in order to pass the man and woman at a little distance unobserved. No; I was not mistaken. The
woman was Mary Simms, though without any trace

of all her former simple-minded airs; Mary Simms,
no longer in her humble attire, but flaunting in all
the finery of overdone fashion. She wore an air
of reckless joyousness in her face; and yet, spite
of that, I pitied her. It was clear she had fallen
on the evil ways of bettered fortune—bettered,
alas! for the worse.

I had an excuse now, in my own mind, for my
continued pursuit, without deeming myself an utter
madman—the excuse of curiosity to know the des-
tiny of one with whom I had been formerly familiar, and in whom I had taken an interest. Presently the game I was hunting down stopped at the
door of the Grand Café. After a little discussion
they entered. It was a public place of entertainment; there was no reason why I should not enter
also. I found my way to the first floor. They
were already seated at a table, Mary holding the
carte in her hand. They were about to dine. Why
should not I dine there too? There was but one
little objection,—I had an engagement to dinner.
But the strange impulse which overpowered me,
and seemed leading me on step by step, spite of
myself, quickly overruled all the dictates of propriety toward my intended hosts. Could I not
send a prettily devised apology? I glided past the
couple, with my head averted, seeking a table, and
I was unobserved by my old acquaintance. I was
too agitated to eat, but I made a semblance, and
little heeded the air of surprise and almost disgust
on the bewildered face of the waiter as he bore
away the barely touched dishes. I was in a very
fever of impatience and doubt what next to do.
They still sat on, in evident enjoyment of their

meal and their constant draughts of sparkling wine. My impatience was becoming almost unbearable when the man at last rose. The woman seemed to have uttered some expostulation, for he turned at the door and said somewhat harshly aloud, "Nonsense; only one game and I shall be back. The waiter will give you a paper—a magazine—something to while away the time." And he left the room for the billiard-table, as I surmised.

Now was my opportunity. After a little hesitation, I rose, and planted myself abruptly on the vacant seat before the woman.

"Mary," I said.

She started, with a little exclamation of alarm, and dropped the paper she had held. She knew me at once.

"Master John!" she exclaimed, using the familiar term still given me when I was long past boyhood; and then, after a lengthened gaze, she turned away her head. I was embarrassed at first how to address her.

"Mary," I said at last, "I am grieved to see you thus."

"Why should you be grieved for me?" she retorted, looking at me sharply, and speaking in a tone of impatient anger. "I am happy as I am."

"I don't believe you," I replied.

She again turned away her head.

"Mary," I pursued, "can you doubt, that, spite of all, I have still a strong interest in the companion of my youth?"

She looked at me almost mournfully, but did not speak. At that moment I probably grew pale; for suddenly that chilly fit seized me again, and my

13

forehead became clammy. That voice sounded
again in my ear: "Speak of him!" were the words
it uttered. Mary gazed on me with surprise, and
yet I was assured that *she* had not heard that voice,
so plain to me. She evidently mistook the nature
of my visible emotion.

"O Master John!" she stammered, with tears
gathering in her eyes, reverting again to that name
of bygone times, "if you had loved me then—if
you had consoled my true affection with one word
of hope, one look of loving-kindness—if you had not
spurned and crushed me, I should not have been
what I am now."

I was about to make some answer to this burst
of unforgotten passion, when the voice came again:
"Speak of him!"

"You have loved others since," I remarked, with
a coldness which seemed cruel to myself. "You
love *him* now." And I nodded my head toward
the door by which the man had disappeared.

"Do I?" she said, with a bitter smile. "Perhaps;
who knows?"

"And yet no good can come to you from a
connection with that man," I pursued.

"Why not? He adores me, and he is free," was
her answer, given with a little triumphant air.

"Yes," I said, "I know he is free: he has lately
lost his wife. He has made good his claim to the
sum for which he insured her life."

Mary grew deadly pale. "How did you learn
this? what do you know of him?" she stammered.

I had no reply to give. She scanned my face
anxiously for some time; then in a low voice she
added, "What do you suspect?"

I was still silent, and only looked at her fixedly. "You do not speak," she pursued nervously. "Why do you not speak? Ah, you know more than you would say! Master John, Master John, you might set my tortured mind at rest, and clear or confirm those doubts which *will* come into my poor head, spite of myself. Speak out—O, do speak out!"

"Not here; it is impossible," I replied, looking around. The room as the hour advanced, was becoming more thronged with guests, and the full tables gave a pretext for my reticence, when in truth I had nothing to say.

"Will you come and see me—will you?" she asked with earnest entreaty.

I nodded my head.

"Have you a pocketbook? I will write you my address; and you will come—yes, I am sure you will come!" she said in an agitated way.

I handed her my pocketbook and pencil; she wrote rapidly.

"Between the hours of three and five," she whispered, looking uneasily at the door; "*he* is sure not to be at home."

I rose; Mary held out her hand to me, then withdrew it hastily with an air of shame, and the tears sprang into her eyes again. I left the room hurriedly, and met her companion on the stairs.

That same evening, in the solitude of my own room, I pondered over the little event of the day. I had calmed down from my state of excitement. The living apparition of Mary Simms occupied my mind almost to the exclusion of the terrors of the ghostly voice which had haunted me, and my own fears of coming insanity. In truth, what was that man to me? Nothing. What did his doings matter to such a perfect stranger as myself? Nothing. His connection with Mary Simms was our only link; and in what should that affect me? Nothing again. I debated with myself whether it were not foolish of me to comply with my youthful companion's request to visit her; whether it were not imprudent in me to take any further interest in the lost woman; whether there were not even danger in seeking to penetrate mysteries which were no concern of mine. The resolution to which I came pleased me, and I said aloud, " No, I will not go!"

At the same moment came again the voice like an awful echo to my words—" Go!" It came so suddenly and so imperatively, almost without any previous warning of the usual shudder, that the shock was more than I could bear. I believe I fainted; I know I found myself, when I came to consciousness, in my arm-chair, cold and numb, and my candles had almost burned down into their sockets.

The next morning I was really ill. A sort of low fever seemed to have prostrated me, and I would have willingly seized so valid a reason for disobeying, at least for that day—for some days, perhaps —the injunction of that ghostly voice. But all that morning it never left me. My fearful chilly fit was of constant recurrence, and the words " Go! go! go!" were murmured so perpetually in my ears —the sound was one of such urgent entreaty—that all force of will gave way completely. Had I remained in that lone room, I should have gone wholly mad. As yet, to my own feelings, I was but partially out of my senses.

I dressed hastily; and, I scarce know how—by no effort of my own will, it seemed to me—I was in the open air. The address of Mary Simms was in a street not far from my own suburb. Without any power of reasoning, I found myself before the door of the house. I knocked, and asked a slip-shod girl who opened the door to me for "Miss Simms." She knew no such person, held a brief shrill colloquy with some female in the back-parlor, and, on coming back, was about to shut the door in my face, when a voice from above—the voice of her I sought—called down the stairs, "Let the gentleman come up!"

I was allowed to pass. In the front drawing-room I found Mary Simms.

"They do not know me under that name," she said with a mournful smile, and again extended, then withdrew, her hand.

"Sit down," she went on to say, after a nervous pause. "I am alone now; and I adjure you, if you have still one latent feeling of old kindness for me, explain your words of yesterday to me."

I muttered something to the effect that I had no explanation to give. No words could be truer; I had not the slightest conception what to say.

"Yes, I am sure you have; you must, you will," pursued Mary excitedly; "you have some knowledge of that matter."

"What matter?" I asked.

"Why, the insurance," she replied impatiently. "You know well what I mean. My mind has been distracted about it. Spite of myself, terrible suspicions have forced themselves on me. No; I don't mean that," she cried, suddenly checking herself and changing her tone; "don't heed what I said; it was madness in me to say what I did. But do, do, do tell me all you know."

The request was a difficult one to comply with, for I knew nothing. It is impossible to say what might have been the end of this strange interview, in which I began to feel myself an unwilling impostor; but suddenly Mary started.

"The noise of the latchkey in the lock!" she cried, alarmed; "He has returned; he must not see you; you must come another time. Here, here, be quick! I'll manage him."

And before I could utter another word she had pushed me into the back drawing-room and closed the door. A man's step on the stairs; then voices. The man was begging Mary to come out with him, as the day was so fine. She excused herself; he would hear no refusal. At last she appeared to consent, on condition that the man would assist at her toilet. There was a little laughter, almost hysterical on the part of Mary, whose voice evidently quivered with trepidation.

Presently both mounted the upper stairs. Then the thought stuck me that I had left my hat in the front room—a sufficient cause for the woman's alarm. I opened the door cautiously, seized my hat, and was about to steal down the stairs, when I was again spellbound by that numb cold.

"Stay!" said the voice. I staggered back to the other room with my hat, and closed the door.

Presently the couple came down. Mary was probably relieved by discovering that my hat was no longer there, and surmised that I had departed; for I heard her laughing as they went down the lower flight. Then I heard them leave the house.

I was alone in that back drawing-room. Why? what did I want there? I was soon to learn. I felt the chill invisible presence near me; and the voice said, "Search!"

The room belonged to the common representative class of back drawing-rooms in "apartments" of the better kind. The only one unfamiliar piece of furniture was an old Indian cabinet; and my eye naturally fell on that. As I stood and looked at it with a strange unaccountable feeling of fascination, again came the voice—"Search!"

I shuddered and obeyed. The cabinet was firmly locked; there was no power of opening it except by burglarious infraction; but still the voice said, "Search!"

A thought suddenly struck me, and I turned the cabinet from its position against the wall. Behind, the woodwork had rotted, and in many portions fallen away, so that the inner drawers were visible. What could my ghostly monitor mean—that I should open those drawers? I would not do such a deed of petty treachery. I turned defiantly, and addressing myself to the invisible as if it were a living creature by my side, I cried, "I must not, will not, do such an act of baseness."

The voice replied, "Search!"

I might have known that, in my state of what I deemed insanity, resistance was in vain. I grasped the most accessible drawer from behind, and pulled it toward me. Uppermost within it lay letters: they were addressed to "Captain Cameron,"— "Captain George Cameron." That name!—the name of Julia's husband, the man with whom she had eloped; for it was he who was the object of my pursuit.

My shuddering fit became so strong that I could scarce hold the papers; and "Search!" was repeated in my ear.

Below the letters lay a small book in a limp black cover. I opened this book with trembling hand; it was filled with manuscript—Julia's well-known handwriting.

"Read!" muttered the voice. I read. There were long entries by poor Julia of her daily life; complaints of her husband's unkindness, neglect, then cruelty. I turned to the last pages: her hand had grown very feeble now, and she was very ill. "George seems kinder now," she wrote; "he brings me all my medicines with his own hand." Later on: "I am dying; I know I am dying: he has poisoned me. I saw him last night through the curtains pour something in my cup; I saw it in his evil eye. I would not drink; I will drink no more; but I feel that I must die."

These were the last words. Below were written, in a man's bold hand, the words "Poor fool!"

This sudden revelation of poor Julia's death and dying thoughts unnerved me quite. I grew colder in my whole frame than ever.

"Take it!" said her voice. I took the book, pushed back the cabinet into its place against the wall, and, leaving that fearful room, stole down the stairs with trembling limbs, and left the house with all the feelings of a guilty thief.

For some days I perused my poor lost Julia's diary again and again. The whole revelation of

her sad life and sudden death led but to one conclusion,—she had died of poison by the hands of
her unworthy husband. He had insured her life,
and then——

It seemed evident·to me that Mary Simms had
vaguely shared suspicions of the same foul deed.
On my own mind came conviction. But what could
I do next? how bring this evil man to justice? what
proof would be deemed to exist in those writings?
I was bewildered, weak, irresolute. Like Hamlet,
I shrank back and temporized. But I was not
feigning madness; my madness seemed but all too
real for me. During all this period the wailing of
that wretched voice in my ear was almost incessant.
O, I must have been mad!

I wandered about restlessly, like the haunted
thing I had become. One day I had come uncon-
sciously and without purpose into Oxford Street.
My troubled thoughts were suddenly broken in
upon by the solicitations of a beggar. With a
heart hardened against begging impostors, and
under the influence of the shock rudely given to
my absorbing dreams, I answered more hardly than
was my wont. The man heaved a heavy sigh, and
sobbed forth, "Then Heaven help me!" I caught
sight of him before he turned away. He was a
ghastly object, with fever in his hollow eyes and
sunken cheeks, and fever on his dry, chapped lips.
But I knew, or fancied I knew, the tricks of the
trade, and I was obdurate. Why, I asked myself,
should the cold shudder come over me at such a
moment? But it was so strong on me as to make
me shake all over. It came—that maddening
voice. "Succor!" it said now. I had become so

accustomed already to address the ghostly voice
that I cried aloud, " Why, Julia, why?" I saw
people laughing in my face at this strange cry, and
I turned in the direction in which the beggar had
gone. I just caught sight of him as he was tottering down a street toward Soho. I determined to
have pity for this once, and followed the poor man.
He led me on through I know not what streets.
His steps was hurried now. In one street I lost
sight of him; but I felt convinced he must have
turned into a dingy court. I made inquiries, but
for a time received only rude jeering answers from
the rough men and women whom I questioned. At
last a little girl informed me that I must mean the
strange man who lodged in the garret of a house
she pointed out to me. It was an old dilapidated
building, and I had much repugnance on entering it.
But again I was no master of my will. I mounted
some creaking stairs to the top of the house, until
I could go no further. A shattered door was
open; I entered a wretched garret; the object of my
search lay now on a bundle of rags on the bare floor.
He opened his wild eyes as I approached.

" I have come to succor," I said, using uncon-
sciously the word of the voice; " what ails you?"

" Ails me?" gasped the man; " hunger, starva-
tion, fever."

I was horrified. Hurrying to the top of the
stairs, I shouted till I had roused the attention of
an old woman. I gave her money to bring me food
and brandy, promising her a recompense for her
trouble.

" Have you no friends?" I asked the wretched
man as I returned.

"None," he said feebly. Then as the fever rose in his eyes and even flushed his pallid face, he said excitedly, "I had a master once—one I perilled my soul for. He knows I am dying; but, spite of all my letters, he will not come. He wants me dead, he wants me dead—and his wish is coming to pass now."

"Cannot I find him—bring him here?" I asked.

The man stared at me, shook his head, and at last, as if collecting his faculties with much exertion, muttered, "Yes; it is a last hope; perhaps you may, and I can be revenged on him at least. Yes revenged. I have threatened him already." And the fellow laughed a wild laugh.

"Control yourself," I urged, kneeling by his side; "give me his name—his address."

"Captain George Cameron," he gasped, and then fell back.

"Captain George Cameron!" I cried. "Speak! what of him?"

But the man's senses seemed gone; he only muttered incoherently. The old woman returned with the food and spirits. I had found one honest creature in that foul region. I gave her money—provide her more if she would bring a doctor. She departed on her new errand. I raised the man's head, moistened his lips with the brandy, and then poured some of the spirit down his throat. He gulped at it eagerly, and opened his eyes; but he still raved incoherently, "I did not do it, it was he. He made me buy the poison; he dared not risk the danger himself, the coward! I knew what he meant to do with it, and yet I did not speak; I was her murderer too. Poor Mrs. Cameron! poor

Mrs. Cameron! do you forgive?—can you forgive?"
And the man screamed aloud and stretched out his
arms as if to fright away a phantom.

I had drunk in every word, and knew the
meaning of those broken accents well. Could I
have found at last the means of bringing justice on
the murderer's head? But the man was raving in a
delirium, and I was obliged to hold him with all
my strength. A step on the stairs. Could it be
the medical man I had sent for? That would be
indeed a blessing. A man entered—it was
Cameron!

He came in jauntily, with the words, "How now,
Saunders, you rascal! What more do you want to
get out of me?"

He started at the sight of a stranger.

I rose from my kneeling posture like an accusing
spirit. I struggled for calm; but passion beyond
my control mastered me, and was I not a mad-
man? I seized him by the throat, with the words,
"Murderer! poisoner! where is Julia?" He shook
me off violently.

"And who the devil are you, sir?" he cried.

"That murdered woman's cousin!" I rushed at
him again.

"Lying hound!" he shouted, and grappled me.
His strength was far beyond mine. He had his
hand on my throat; a crimson darkness was in my
eyes; I could not see, I could not hear; there was
a torrent of sound pouring in my ears. Suddenly
his grasp relaxed. When I recovered my sight, I
saw the murderer struggling with the fever-stricken
man, who had risen from the floor, and seized him
from behind. This unexpected diversion saved my

life; but the ex-groom was soon thrown back on the ground.

"Captain George Cameron," I cried, "kill me, but you will only heap another murder on your head!"

He advanced on me with something glittering in his hand. Without a word he came and stabbed at me; but at the same moment I darted at him a heavy blow. What followed was too confused for clear remembrance. I saw—no, I will say I fancied that I saw—the dim form of Julia Staunton standing between me and her vile husband. Did he see the vision too? I cannot say. He reeled back, and fell heavily to the floor. Maybe it was only my blow that felled him. Then came confusion—a dream of a crowd of people—policemen—muttered accusations. I had fainted from the wound in my arm.

Captain George Cameron was arrested. Saunders recovered, and lived long enough to be the principal witness on his trial. The murderer was found guilty. Poor Julia's diary, too, which I had abstracted, told fearfully against him. But he contrived to escape the gallows; he had managed to conceal poison on his person, and he was found dead in his cell. Mary Simms I never saw again. I once received a little scrawl, "I am at peace now, Master John. God bless you!"

I have had no more hallucinations since that time; the voice has never come again. I found out poor Julia's grave, and, as I stood and wept by its side, the cold shudder came over me for the last time. Who shall tell me whether I was once really mad, or whether I was not?

DOCTOR FEVERSHAM'S STORY.

DOCTOR FEVERSHAM'S STORY.

"I HAVE made a point all my life," said the doctor, "of believing nothing of the kind."

Much ghost-talk by firelight had been going on in the library at Fordwick Chase, when Doctor Feversham made this remark.

"As much as to say," observed Amy Fordwick, "that you are afraid to tackle the subject, because you pique yourself on being strong-minded, and are afraid of being convinced against your will."

"Not precisely, young lady. A man convinced against his will is in a different state of mind from mine in matters like these. But it is true that cases in which the supernatural element appears at first sight to enter are so numerous in my profession, that I prefer accepting only the solutions of science, so far as they go, to entering on any wild speculations which it would require more time than I should care to devote to them to trace to their origin."

"But without entering fully into the why and wherefore, how can you be sure that the proper treatment is observed in the numerous cases of mental hallucination which must come under your notice?" inquired Latimer Fordwick, who was studying for the Bar.

14   209

"I content myself, my young friend, with following the rules laid down for such cases, and I generally find them successful," answered the old Doctor.

"Then you admit that cases have occurred within your knowledge of which the easiest apparent solution could be one which involved a belief in supernatural agencies?" persisted Latimer, who was rather prolix and pedantic in his talk.

"I did not say so," said the Doctor.

"But of course he meant us to infer it," said Amy. "Now, my dear old Doctor, do lay aside professional dignity, and give us one good ghost-story out of your personal experience. I believe you have been dying to tell one for the last hour, if you would only confess it."

"I would rather not help to fill that pretty little head with idle fancies, dear child," answered the old man, looking fondly at Amy, who was his especial pet and darling.

"Nonsense! You know I am even painfully unimaginative and matter-of-fact; and as for idle fancies, is it an idle fancy to think you like to please me?" said Amy coaxingly.

"Well, after all, you have been frightening each other with so many thrilling tales for the last hour or two, that I don't suppose I should do much harm by telling you a circumstance which happened to me when I was a young man, and has always rather puzzled me."

A murmur of approval ran round the party. All disposed themselves to listen; and Doctor Feversham, after a prefatory pinch of snuff, began.

"In my youth I resided for some time with a

family in the north of England, in the double capacity of secretary and physician. While I was
going through the hospitals of Paris I became
acquainted with my employer, whom I will call
Sir James Collingham, under rather peculiar circumstances, which have nothing to do with my
story. He had an only daughter, who was about
sixteen when I first entered the family, and it was
on her account that Sir James wished to have some
person with a competent knowledge of medicine
and physiology as one of his household. Miss
Collingham was subject to fits of a very peculiar
kind, which threw her into a sort of trance, lasting
from half an hour to three or even four days, according to the severity of the visitation. During
these attacks she occasionally displayed that extraordinary phenomenon which goes by the name
of clairvoyance. She saw scenes and persons who
were far distant, and described them with wonderful accuracy. Though quite unconscious of all outward things, and apparently in a state of the deepest insensibility, she would address remarks to
those present which bore reference to the thoughts
then occupying their minds, though they had given
them no outward expression; and her remarks
showed an insight into matters which had perhaps
been carefully kept secret, which might truly be
termed preternatural. Under these circumstances,
Sir James was very unwilling to bring her into
contact with strangers when it could possibly be
avoided; and the events which first brought us
together, having also led to my treating Miss Collingham rather successfully in a severe attack of
her malady, induced her father to offer me a posi-

tion in his household which, as a young, friendless man, I was very willing to accept.

"Collingham - Westmore was a very ancient house of great extent, and but indifferently kept in repair. The country surrounding it is of great natural beauty, thinly inhabited, and, especially at the time I speak of, before railways had penetrated so far north, somewhat lonely and inaccessible. A group of small houses clustered round the village church of Westmorton, distant about three miles from the mansion of the Collingham family; and a solitary posting-house, on what was then the great north road, could be reached by a horseman in about an hour, though the only practicable road for carriages was at least fifteen miles from the highway to Collingham - Westmore. Wild and lovely in the eyes of an admirer of nature were the hills and 'cloughs' among which I pursued my botanical studies for many a long, silent summer day. My occupations at the mansion —everybody called it the mansion, and I must do so from force of habit, though it sounds rather like a house-agent's advertisement — were few and light; the society was not particularly to my taste, and the fine old library only attracted me on rainy days, of which, truth to say, we had our full share.

"The Collingham family circle comprised a maiden aunt of Sir James, Miss Patricia, a stern and awful specimen of the female sex in its fossil state; her ward, Miss Henderson, who, having long passed her pupilage, remained at Collingham-Westmore in the capacity of gouvernante and companion to the young heiress; the heiress aforesaid, and myself. A priest—did I say that the Collinghams still professed the old religion?—came on Sundays and holydays to celebrate mass in the gloomy old chapel; but neighbors there were none, and only about half-a-dozen times during the four years I was an inmate of the mansion were strangers introduced into the family party."

"How dreadfully dull it must have been!" exclaimed Amy sympathetically.

"It *was* dull," answered the Doctor. "Even with my naturally cheerful disposition, and the course of study with which I methodically filled up all my leisure hours except those devoted to out-of-door exercise, the gloom of the old mansion weighed upon me till I sometimes felt that I must give up my situation at all risks, and return to the world, though it were to struggle with poverty and friendlessness.

"There was no lack of dismal legends and superstitions connected with the mansion, and every trifling circumstance that occurred was twisted into an omen or presage, whether of good or evil, by the highly wrought fancy of Miss Patricia. These absurdities, together with the past grandeur of their house, and the former glories of their religion, formed the staple subjects of conversation when the family was assembled; and as I became more intimately acquainted with the state of my patient, I felt convinced that the atmosphere of gloomy superstition in which she had been reared had fostered, even if it had not altogether been the cause of, her morbid mental and bodily condition.

"Among the many legends connected with the mansion, one seemed to have a peculiar fascination for Miss Collingham, perhaps because it was the most ghastly and repulsive. One wing of the house was held to be haunted by the spirit of an ancestress of the family, who appeared in the shape of a tall woman, with one hand folded in her white robe and the other pointing upward. It was said, that in a room at the end of the haunted wing this lady had been foully murdered by her jealous husband. The window of the apartment overhung the wild wooded side of one of the 'cloughs' common in the country; and tradition averred that the victim was thrown from this window by her murderer. As she caught hold of the sill in a last frantic struggle for life, he severed her hand at the wrist, and the mutilated body fell, with one fearful shriek, into the depth below. Since then, a white shadowy form has forever been sitting at the fatal window, or wandering along the deserted passages of the haunted wing with the bleeding stump folded in her robe; and in moments of danger or approaching death to any member of the Collingham family, the same long, wild shriek rises slowly from the wooded cliff and peals through the mansion; while to different individuals of the house, a pale hand has now and then been visible, laid on themselves or some other of the family, a never-failing omen of danger or death.

"I need not tell you how false and foolish all this dreary superstition appeared to me; and I exerted all my powers of persuasion to induce Miss Patricia to dwell less on these and similar themes in the presence of Miss Collingham. But there seemed to be something in the very air of the gloomy old mansion which fostered such delusions;

for when I spoke to Father O'Connor the priest, and urged on him the pernicious effect which was thus produced on my patient's mind, I found him as fully imbued with the spirit of credulity as the most hysterical housemaid of them all. He solemnly declared to me that he had himself repeatedly seen the pale lady sitting at the fatal window, when on his way to and from his home beyond the hills; and moreover, that on the death of Lady Collingham, which occurred at her daughter's birth, he had heard the long, shrill death-scream echo through the mansion while engaged in the last offices of the Church by the bedside of the dying lady.

"So I found it impossible to fight single-handed against these adverse influences, and could only endeavor to divert the mind of my patient into more healthy channels of thought. In this I succeeded perfectly. She became an enthusiastic botanist, and our rambles in search of the rare and lovely specimens which were to be found among the woods and moors surrounding her dwelling did more for her health, both of body and mind, than all the medical skill I could bring to bear on her melancholy case.

"Four years had elapsed since I first took up my abode at Collingham-Westmore. Miss Collingham had grown from a sickly child into a singularly graceful young woman, full of bright intelligence, eager for information, and with scarcely an outward trace remaining of her former fragile health. Still those mysterious swoons occasionally visited her, forming an insurmountable obstacle to her mingling in general sociey, which she was in all

other respects so well fitted to adorn. They occurred without any warning or apparent cause;
one moment she would be engaged in animated
conversation, and the next, white and rigid as a
statue, she would fall back in her chair insensible
to all outward objects, but rapt and carried away
into a world of her own, whose visions she would
sometimes describe in glowing language, although
she retained no recollection whatever of them when
she returned, as suddenly and at as uncertain a
period, to her normal condition. On one of these
occasions we were sitting, after dinner, in a large
apartment called the summer dining-room. Fruit
and wine were on the table, and the last red beams
of the setting sun lighted up the distant woods,
which were in the first flush of their autumn glory.
I turned to remark on the beautiful effect of light
to Miss Collingham, and at the very moment I did
so she fell back in one of her strange swoons. But
instead of the death-like air which her features
usually assumed, a lovely smile lighted them up,
and an expression of ecstasy made her beauty appear for the moment almost superhuman. Slowly
she raised her right hand, and pointed in the direction of the setting sun. 'He is coming,' she said
in soft, clear tones; 'life and light are coming
with him,—life and light and liberty!'

"Her hand fell gently by her side; the rapt expression faded from her countenance, and the usual
death-like blank overspread it. This trance passed
away like others, and by midnight the house was
profoundly still. Soon after that hour a vociferous
peal at the great hall-bell roused most of the inmates from sleep. My rooms were in a distant

quarter of the house, and a door opposite to that
of my bedroom led to the haunted wing, but was
always kept locked. I started up on hearing a
second ring, and looked out, in hopes of seeing a
servant pass, and ascertaining the cause of this
unusual disturbance. I saw no one, and after listening for a while to the opening of the hall-door,
and the sound of distant voices, I made up my
mind that I should be sent for if wanted, and re-
entered my room. As I was closing the door, I
was rather startled to see a tall object, of grayish-
white color and indistinct form, issue from the
gallery whose door, as I said before, had always
been locked in my recollection. For a moment I
felt as though rooted to the spot, and a strange
sensation crept over me. The next, all trace of
the appearance had vanished, and I persuaded
myself that what I had seen must have been some
effect of light from the open door of my room.

"The cause of the nightly disturbance appeared
at breakfast on the following morning in the shape
of a remarkably handsome young man, who was
introduced by Sir James as his nephew, Don Luis
de Cabral, the son of an only sister long dead, who
had married a Spaniard of high rank. Don Luis
showed but little trace of his southern parentage.
If I may so express it, all the depth and warmth
of coloring in that portion of his blood which he
inherited from his Spanish ancestors came out in
the raven-black hair and large lustrous dark eyes,
which impressed you at once with their uncommon
beauty. For the rest, he was a fine well-grown
young man, no darker in complexion than an Eng-
lishman might well be, and with a careless, happy

boyishness of manner, which won immediately on
the regard of strangers, and rendered his presence
in the house like that of a perpetual sunbeam.
We all wondered, after a little while, what we had
done before Luis came among us. He was as a
son to Sir James; Miss Patricia softened to this
new and pleasing interest in her colorless existence
as I could not have believed it was in her fossilized
nature to do; Miss Henderson became animated,
almost young, under the reviving influence of the
youth and joyousness of our new inmate; and I
own that I speedily attached myself with a warm
and affectionate regard to the happy, unselfish nature that seemed to brighten all who came near it.

"But the most remarkable effect of the presence
of Don Luis de Cabral among us was visible in
Miss Collingham. 'Love at first sight,' often considered as a mere phrase, was, in the case of these
two young creatures, an unmistakable reality.
From the moment of their first meeting, the cousins were mutually drawn toward each other; and
seeing the bright and wonderful change wrought
by the presence of Don Luis in Blanche Collingham, I could not but remember, with the interest
that attaches to a curious psychological phenomenon, the words she uttered in her trance on the
eve of his arrival. 'Life, light, and liberty,' indeed, appeared given to all that was best and
brightest in her nature. Her health improved vis-
ibly, and her beauty, always touching, became ra-
diant in its full development. My duties toward
her were now merely nominal; and when, about
two months later, Sir James announced to me her
approaching marriage, and confessed that it was

with this object he had invited Don Luis to come and make the acquaintance of his English relations, the strong opinions I entertained against the marriage of first cousins, and also on the especial inadvisability of any project of marriage in the case of Miss Collingham, could not prevent my hearty rejoicing in the fair prospect of happiness in which two persons who deeply interested me were indulging.

"Winter set in early and severely that year among our northern hills, and with a view to Blanche's removal from its withering influence, which I always considered prejudicial to her, the preparations for the marriage were hurried on, and the ceremony was fixed to take place about the middle of December. The travelling - carriage which was to convey the young couple on their way southward was to arrive at the nearest railway-station—then more than thirty miles distant —a week before the marriage; and as some important portions of the trousseau, together with a valuable package of jewels intended by Don Luis as presents for his bride, were expected at the same time, the young man announced his intention of riding across the hills to ——, in order to superintend the conveyance of the carriage and its contents along the rough mountain roads that it must traverse.

" We were all sitting around the great fireplace in the winter parlor on the evening before his departure. Miss Collingwood had been languid and depressed throughout the day, and often adverted to the long wintry ride he was to undertake in a strain of apprehension at which Don Luis laughed gayly. To divert her mind, he recounted various adventures which had befallen him in foreign lands, with a vigorous simplicity of description which enchained her attention and interested us all.

"Suddenly, so sitting, Miss Collingham leaned forward, and in a changed, eager voice exclaimed, 'Luis, take away your hand from your throat!'

"We looked. Luis' hands were lying one over the other on his knee in a careless attitude that was habitual to him.

"'Take it away, I say! Oh, take it away!'

Miss Collingham started to her feet as she uttered these words almost in a shriek, and then fell back rigid and senseless, her outstretched hand still pointing to her betrothed.

"The fit was a severe one, but by morning it had yielded to remedies, and Luis set off early on his ride, to make the most of the short daylight, and intending to return with the carriage on the morrow. All that day Miss Collingham remained in a half-conscious state. It was a dreary day of gloom, with a piercing north wind, and toward evening the snow began to fall in those close, compact flakes which forebode a heavy storm. We were glad to think that Luis must have reached his destination before it began; but when the next morning dawned on a wide expanse of snow, and the air was still thick with fast-falling flakes, it was feared that the state of the roads would preclude all hope of the arrival of the carriage on that day.

"My patient took no heed of the untoward state of the weather. She was still in a drowsy condition, very unlike that which usually succeeded her attacks, and Miss Henderson, who had watched by her through the night, told me she spoke more than once in a strange, excited manner, as though carrying on a conversation with some one whom she appeared to see by her bedside. As the good lady, however, could give but a very imperfect and incoherent account of what had passed, I was left in some doubt as to whether Miss Collingham had seen more or Miss Henderson less than there really was to be seen, as I had before had reason to believe that she was not a very vigilant nurse.

"So the hours went on, and night closed in. Sir James began to feel some uneasiness at the non-appearance, not only of Don Luis, but also of the priest, who was to have arrived at Collingham-Westmore on that day.

"On questioning some of the servants who had been out of the house, the absence of Father O'Connor at least was satisfactorily accounted for: they all declared that it would be quite impossible for those best acquainted with the hills to find their way across them in the blinding drifts which had never ceased throughout the day. We concluded that Father O'Connor and Don Luis were alike storm-stayed, and had no remedy but patience.

"Late in the evening—it must have been near midnight—I was in Miss Collingham's dressing-room with Miss Patricia, who intended to watch by her through the night. We were talking by the fire, of the snow-storm which still continued, and of the hindrance it might prove to the marriage—the day fixed for which was now less than a week distant—when we heard a voice in the adjoining room, where we imagined the object of our care to be sleeping. We went in. Miss Collingham was sitting up in bed, her eyes wide open, in one of her rigid fits. She was speaking rapidly in a low tone, unlike her usual voice.

"'You cannot get through all that snow,' she said. 'Get help; there are men not far off with spades. Oh, be careful! You are off the road! Stop, stop! that is the way to Armstrong's Clough. Does not the postboy know the road? He is bewildered. I tell you it is madness to go on. See, one of the horses has fallen; he kicks—he will hit you! Oh, how dark it is! And the snow covers your lantern, and you cannot see the edge. Now the horse is up again, but he cannot go on. Do not beat him, Luis; it is not his fault, poor beast; the snow is too thick, and you are on rough ground. Now he rears—he backs—the other one backs also—the wheel of the carriage is over the edge—ah!'

"The scream with which these wild, hurried words ended seemed to be taken up and echoed from a distance. Miss Patricia stared at me with a ghastly white face of horror, and I felt my blood curdle as that long, shrill, unearthly shriek pealed through the silent passages. It grew louder and nearer, and seemed to sweep through the room, dying away in the opposite direction. Miss Patricia fell forward without a word in a dead faint.

"I looked at Miss Collingham; she had not moved, or shown any sign of hearing or heeding that awful sound. In a few seconds the room was filled with terrified women, roused from their sleep by

the weird cry which rang through the house. Miss
Patricia was conveyed by some of them to her own
room, where, after much difficulty, we restored her
to consciousness. Her first act was to grasp me by
the arm.

"'Mr. Feversham, for the love of the Holy Vir-
gin do not leave me! I have seen that which I
cannot look upon and live.'

. "I soothed her as best I might, and at last persuaded her to allow me to leave her with her own
maid in order to visit my other patient, promising
to return shortly.

"I found no change whatever in Miss Collingham. Sir James was in the room trying to estab-
lish some degree of calmness and order among the
terrified women. We succeeded in persuading
most of them to take a restorative and return to
bed, and leaving two of the most self-possessed to
watch beside Miss Collingham, who was still completely insensible, we went together to Miss Patricia's room:

"'Brother, I have seen her!' she exclaimed on
Sir James' entrance.

"'Seen who, my dear Patricia?'

"'The pale lady—the spectre of our house,'·she
replied, shuddering from head to foot. 'She
passed through the room, her hand upraised, and
the blood-spots on her garment. Oh, James! my
time is come, and Father O'Connor is not here.'

"Sir James did not attempt to combat his sister's
superstitious terrors, but appeared, on the contrary,
almost as deeply impressed as herself, and questioned her closely about the apparition. Her answers led to some mention of the strange vision

which Miss Collingham was describing in her trance just before the scream was heard. At Sir James' request I put down in writing, as nearly as I could remember, all she had said, and so great was the impression it made on my mind that I believe I recalled her very words. Knowing all we did of her abnormal condition while in a state of trance, it was impossible not to fear that she might have been describing a scene that was actually occurring at the time; and Sir James determined to send out a party, as soon as daylight came, on the road by which Don Luis must arrive.

"'The morning dawned brightly, with a keen frost, and several men were sent off along the road to —— with the first rays of light.

"Some hours afterward Father O'Connor arrived, having made his way with considerable difficulty across the hill. Miss Patricia claimed his first attention, for my unhappy charge remained senseless and motionless as ever.

"After a long conference, he came to me with grave looks.

"'She is at the window this day,' he said, shaking his head sorrowfully, when I had told him my share of the last night's singular experiences. 'The pale lady is there; I saw her as I came by the bridge as plainly as now I see you. We shall have evil tidings of that poor lad before nightfall, or I am strangely mistaken.'

"Evil tidings indeed they were that reached us on the return of some of the exploring-party. They were first attracted from following as nearly as they could the line of road, blocked as it was with drifts of snow by hearing the howling of a dog at some little distance, in the direction of the precipitous ravine which went by the name of 'Armstrong's Clough.' Following the sound, they came upon traces of wheels in the hill-side, where no carriage could have gone had it not been for the deep snow which concealed and smoothed away the inequalities of the ground. These marks were traced here and there till they led to the verge of the precipice, where a struggle had evidently taken place, and masses of snow had been dislodged and fallen into the ravine.

"Looking below, the only thing they could see in the waste of snow was a little dog, who was known to be in the habit of running with the post-horses from ——, which was scraping wildly in the snow and filling the air with its dismal howlings. A considerable circuit had to be made before the bottom of the clough could be reached, and then the whole tragedy was revealed. There lay the broken carriage, the dead horses, and two stiffened corpses under the snow, that had drifted over and around them.

"I need not pursue the melancholy story; I was an old fool for telling it to you," said the Doctor.

"But Miss Collingham—what became of her?" asked an eager listener.

"Well, she did not recover," answered the Doctor with a slight trembling in his voice. "It was a sad matter altogether; and within a short time she lay beside her betrothed in the family vault below the chapel. Sir James broke up his establishment and went abroad, and I never saw any of the family again."

"And what did you do, Doctor?"

"I went to London, to seek my fortune as best I might; and I hope you may all prosper as well, my young friends."

"And is it all really true?" asked Amy, who had listened with breathless attention.

"That is the worst of it; it really is," said the Doctor.

THE SECRET OF THE TWO PLASTER CASTS.

THE SECRET OF THE TWO PLASTER CASTS.

YEARS before the accession of her Majesty Queen Victoria, and yet at not so remote a date as to be utterly beyond the period to which the reminiscences of our middle-aged readers extend, it happened that two English gentlemen sat at table on a summer's evening, after dinner, quietly sipping their wine and engaged in desultory conversation. They were both men known to fame. One of them was a sculptor whose statues adorned the palaces of princes, and whose chiselled busts were the pride of half the nobility of his nation; the other was no less renowned as an anatomist and surgeon. The age of the anatomist might have been guessed at fifty, but the guess would have erred on the side of youth by at least ten years. That of the sculptor could scarcely be more than five-and-thirty. A bust of the anatomist, so admirably executed as to present, although in stone, the perfect similitude of life and flesh, stood upon a pedestal opposite to the table at which sat the pair, and at once explained at least one connecting-link of companionship between them. The anatomist was exhibiting for the criticism of his friend a rare gem which he had just drawn from his cabinet: it was

a crucifix magnificently carved in ivory, and incased
in a setting of pure gold.

"The carving, my dear sir," observed Mr. Fiddyes, the sculptor, "is indeed, as you say, exquisite.
The muscles are admirably made out, the flesh well
modelled, wonderfully so for the size and material;
and yet—by the bye, on this point you must know
more than I—the more I think upon the matter,
the more I regard the artistic conception as utterly
false and wrong."

"You speak in a riddle," replied Dr. Carnell;
"but pray go on, and explain."

"It is a fancy I first had in my student-days,"
replied Fiddyes. "Conventionality, not to say a
most proper and becoming reverence, prevents people by no means ignorant from considering the point.
But once think upon it, and you at least, of all men,
must at once perceive how utterly impossible it
would be for a victim nailed upon a cross by hands
and feet to preserve the position invariably displayed in figures of the Crucifixion. Those who so
portray it fail in what should be their most awful
and agonizing effect. Think for one moment, and
imagine, if you can, what would be the attitude of
a man, living or dead, under this frightful torture."

"You startle me," returned the great surgeon,
"not only by the truth of your remarks, but by their
obviousness. It is strange indeed that such a matter
should have so long been overlooked. The more I
think upon it the more the bare idea of actual crucifixion seems to horrify me, though heaven knows
I am accustomed enough to scenes of suffering.
How would you represent such a terrible agony?"

"Indeed I cannot tell," replied the sculptor; "to

guess would be almost vain. The fearful strain upon the muscles, their utter helplessness and inactivity, the frightful swellings, the effect of weight upon the racked and tortured sinews, appal me too much even for speculation."

"But this," replied the surgeon, "one might think a matter of importance, not only to art, but, higher still, to religion itself."

"Maybe so," returned the sculptor. "But perhaps the appeal to the senses through a true representation might be too horrible for either the one or the other."

"Still," persisted the surgeon, "I should like—say for curiosity—though I am weak enough to believe even in my own motive as a higher one—to ascertain the effect from actual observation."

"So should I, could it be done, and of course without pain to the object, which, as a condition, seems to present at the outset an impossibility."

"Perhaps not," mused the anatomist; "I think I have a notion. Stay—we may contrive this matter. I will tell you my plan, and it will be strange indeed if we two cannot manage to carry it out."

The discourse here, owing to the rapt attention of both speakers, assumed a low and earnest tone, but had perhaps better be narrated by a relation of the events to which it gave rise. Suffice it to say that the Sovereign was more than once mentioned during its progress, and in a manner which plainly told that the two speakers each possessed sufficient influence to obtain the assistance of royalty, and that such assistance would be required in their scheme.

"The shades of evening deepened while the two were still conversing. And leaving this scene, let us cast one hurried glimpse at another taking place contemporaneously.

Between Pimlico and Chelsea, and across a canal of which the bed has since been used for the railway terminating at Victoria Station, there was at the time of which we speak a rude timber footway, long since replaced by a more substantial and convenient erection, but then known as the Wooden Bridge. It was named shortly afterward Cutthroat Bridge, and for this reason.

While Mr. Fiddyes and Dr. Carnell were discoursing over their wine, as we have already seen, one Peter Starke, a drunken Chelsea pensioner, was murdering his wife upon the spot we have last indicated. The coincidence was curious.

In those days the punishment of criminals followed closely upon their conviction. The Chelsea pensioner whom we have mentioned was found guilty one Friday and sentenced to die on the following Monday. He was a sad scoundrel, impenitent to the last, glorying in the deeds of slaughter which he had witnessed and acted during the series of campaigns which had ended just previously at Waterloo. He was a tall, well-built fellow enough, of middle age, for his class was not then, as now, composed chiefly of veterans, but comprised many young men, just sufficiently disabled to be unfit for service. Peter Starke, although but slightly wounded, had nearly completed his term of service, and had obtained his pension and presentment to Chelsea Hospital. With his life we have but

little to do, save as regards its close, which we shall
shortly endeavor to describe far more veraciously,
and at some greater length than set forth in the
brief account which satisfied the public of his own
day, and which, as embodied in the columns of the
few journals then appearing, ran thus:

"On Monday last Peter Starke was executed at
Newgate for the murder at the Wooden Bridge,
Chelsea, with four others for various offences.
After he had been hanging only for a few minutes
a respite arrived, but although he was promptly
cut down, life was pronounced to be extinct.   His
body was buried within the prison walls."

Thus far history.   But the conciseness of history
far more frequently embodies falsehood than truth.
Ferhaps the following narration may approach more
nearly to the facts.
     A room within the prison had been, upon that
special occasion and by high authority, allotted to
the use of Dr. Carnell and Mr. Fiddyes, the famous
sculptor, for the purpose of certain investigations
connected with art and science.   In that room Mr.
Fiddyes, while wretched Peter Starke was yet
swinging between heaven and earth, was busily engaged in arranging a variety of implements and
materials, consisting of a large quantity of plaster-
of-Paris, two large pails of water, some tubs, and
other necessaries of the moulder's art.   The room
contained a large deal table, and a wooden cross,
not neatly planed and squared at the angles, but of
thick, narrow, rudely-sawn oaken plank, fixed by
strong, heavy nails.   And while Mr. Fiddyes was

thus occupied, the executioner entered, bearing upon his shoulders the body of the wretched Peter, which he flung heavily upon the table.

"You are sure he is dead?" asked Mr. Fiddyes.

"Dead as a herring," replied the other. "And yet just as warm and limp as if he had only fainted."

"Then go to work at once," relplied the sculptor, as turning his back upon the hangman, he resumed his occupation.

The "work" was soon done. Peter was stripped and nailed upon the timber, which was instantly propped against the wall.

"As fine a one as ever I see," exclaimed the executioner, as he regarded the defunct murderer with an expression of admiration, as if at his own handiwork, in having abruptly demolished such a magnificent animal. "Drops a good bit for'ard, though. Shall I tie him up round the waist, sir?"

"Certainly not," returned the sculptor. "Just rub him well over with this oil, especially his head, and then you can go. Dr. Carnell will settle with you."

"All right, sir."

The fellow did as ordered, and retired without another word; leaving this strange couple, the living and the dead, in that dismal chamber.

Mr. Fiddyes was a man of strong nerve in such matters. He had been too much accustomed to taking posthumous casts to trouble himself with any sentiment of repugnance at his approaching task of taking what is called a "piece-mould" from a body. He emptied a number of bags of the white powdery plaster-of-Paris into one of the larger vessels, poured into it a pail of water, and was carefully stirring up the mass, when a sound of dropping arrested his ear.

Drip, drip.

"There's something leaking," he muttered, as he took a second pail, and emptying it, again stirred the composition.

Drip, drip, drip.

"It's strange," he soliloquized, half aloud. "There is no more water, and yet——"

The sound was heard again.

He gazed at the ceiling; there was no sign of damp. He turned his eyes to the body, and something suddenly caused him a violent start. The murderer was bleeding.

The sculptor, spite of his command over himself, turned pale. At that moment the head of Starke moved—clearly moved. It raised itself convulsively for a single moment; its eyes rolled, and it gavevent to a subdued moan of intense agony. Mr. Fiddyes fell fainting on the floor as Dr. Carnell entered. It needed but a glance to tell the doctor what had happened, even had not Peter just then given vent to another low cry. The surgeon's measures were soon taken. Locking the door, he bore a chair to the wall which supported the body of the malefactor. He drew from his pocket a case of glittering instruments, and with one of these, so small and delicate that it scarcely seemed larger than a needle, he rapidly, but dexterously and firmly, touched Peter just at the back of the neck. There was no wound larger than the head of a small pin, and yet the head fell instantly as though the heart had been pierced. The doctor had divided the spinal cord, and Peter Starke was dead indeed.

A few minutes sufficed to recall the sculptor to his senses. He at first gazed wildly upon the still suspended body, so painfully recalled to life by the rough venesection of the hangman and the subsequent friction of anointing his body to prevent the adhesion of the plaster.

"You need not fear now," said Dr. Carnell; "I assure you he is dead."

"But he *was* alive, surely!"

"Only for a moment, and even that scarcely to be called life—mere muscular contraction, my dear sir, mere muscular contraction."

The sculptor resumed his labor. The body was girt at various circumferences with fine twine, to be afterward withdrawn through a thick coating of plaster, so as to separate the various pieces of the mould, which was at last completed; and after this Dr. Carnell skilfully flayed the body, to enable a second mould to be taken of the entire figure, showing every muscle of the outer layer.

The two moulds were thus taken. It is difficult to conceive more ghastly appearances than they presented. For sculptor's work they were utterly useless; for no artist except the most daring of realists would have ventured to indicate the horrors which they presented. Fiddyes refused to receive them. Dr. Carnell, hard and cruel as he was, for kindness' sake, in his profession, was a gentle, genial father of a family of daughters. He received the casts, and at once consigned them to a garret, to which he forbade access. His youngest daughter, one unfortunate day, during her father's absence, was impelled by feminine curiosity—perhaps a little increased by the prohibition—to enter the mysterious chamber.

Whether she imagined in the pallid figure upon the cross a celestial rebuke for her disobedience, or whether she was overcome by the mere mortal horror of one or both of those dreadful casts, can now never be known. But this is true: she became a maniac.

The writer of this has more than once seen (as, no doubt, have many others) the plaster effigies of Peter Starke, after their removal from Dr. Carnell's to a famous studio near the Regent's Park. It was there that he heard whispered the strange story of their origin. Sculptor and surgeon are now both long since dead, and it is no longer necessary to keep *the secret of the two plaster casts.*

WHAT WAS IT?

WHAT WAS IT?

IT is, I confess, with considerable diffidence that
I approached the strange narrative which I am
about to relate. The events which I purpose
detailing are of so extraordinary a character that I
am quite prepared to meet with an unusual amount
of incredulity and scorn. I accept all such before-
hand. I have, I trust, the literary courage to face
unbelief. I have, after mature consideration, resolved to narrate, in as simple and straightforward
a manner as I can compass, some facts that passed
under my observation, in the month of July last,
and which, in the annals of the mysteries of physical
science, are wholly unparalleled.

I live at No. — Twenty-sixth Street, in New
York. The house is in some respects a curious one.
It has enjoyed for the last two years the reputation
of being haunted. The house is very spacious. A
hall of noble size leads to a large spiral staircase
winding through its centre, while the various apartments are of imposing dimensions. It was built
some fifteen or twenty years since by Mr. A——,
the well-known New York merchant, who five years
ago threw the commercial world into convulsions by
a stupendous bank fraud. Mr. A——, as every one
knows, escaped to Europe, and died not long after,
of a broken heart. Almost immediately after the
news of his decease reached this country and was

16   241

verified, the report spread in Twenty-sixth Street that No. — was haunted. Legal measures had dispossessed the widow of its former owner, and it was inhabited merely by a care-taker and his wife, placed there by the house-agent into whose hands it had passed for purposes of renting or sale. These people declared that they were troubled with unnatural noises. Doors were opened without any visible agency. The remnants of furniture scattered through the various rooms were, during the night, piled one upon the other by unknown hands. Invisible feet passed up and down the stairs in broad daylight, accompanied by the rustle of unseen silk dresses, and the gliding of viewless hands along the massive balusters. The care-taker and his wife declared they would live there no longer. The house-agent laughed, dismissed them, and put others in their place. The noises and supernatural manifestations continued. The neighborhood caught up the story, and the house remained untenanted for three years. Several persons negotiated for it; but, somehow, always before the bargain was closed they heard the unpleasant rumors and declined to treat any further.

It was in this state of things that my landlady, who at that time kept a boarding-house in Bleecker Street, and who wished to move farther up town, conceived the bold idea of renting No. — Twenty-sixth Street. Happening to have in her house rather a plucky and philosophical set of boarders, she laid her scheme before us, stating candidly everything she had heard respecting the ghostly qualities of the establishment to which she wished to remove us. With the exception of two timid persons—a sea-captain and a returned Californian, who immediately gave notice that they would leave—all of Mrs. Moffat's guests declared that they would accompany her in her incursion into the abode of spirits.

Our removal was effected in the month of May, and we were charmed with our new residence.

Of course we had no sooner established ourselves at No. — than we began to expect the ghosts. We absolutely awaited their advent with eagerness. Our dinner conversation was supernatural. I found myself a person of immense importance, it having leaked out that I was tolerably well versed in the history of supernaturalism, and had once written a story the foundation of which was a ghost. If a table or wainscot panel happened to warp when we were assembled in the large drawing-room, there was an instant silence, and every one was prepared for an immediate clanking of chains and a spectral form.

After a month of psychological excitement, it was with the utmost dissatisfaction that we were forced to acknowledge that nothing in the remotest degree approaching the supernatural had manifested itself.

Things were in this state when an incident took place so awful and inexplicable in its character that my reason fairly reels at the bare memory of the occurrence. It was the tenth of July. After dinner was over I repaired, with my friend Dr. Hammond, to the garden to smoke my evening pipe. Independent of certain mental sympathies which existed between the doctor and myself, we were linked together by a vice. We both smoked opium. We knew each other's secret and respected it. We

enjoyed together that wonderful expansion of
thought, that marvellous intensifying of the per-
ceptive faculties, that boundless feeling of existence
when we seem to have points of contact with the
whole universe—in short, that unimaginable spiritual bliss, which I would not surrender for a throne,
and which I hope you, reader, will never—never
taste.

On the evening in question, the tenth of July,
the doctor and myself drifted into an unusually
metaphysical mood. We lit our large meer-
schaums, filled with fine Turkish tobacco, in the
core of which burned a little black nut of opium,
that, like the nut in the fairy tale, held within its
narrow limits wonders beyond the reach of kings;
we paced to and fro, conversing. A strange per-
versity dominated the currents of our thoughts.
They would not flow through the sun-lit channels
into which we strove to divert them. For some
unaccountable reason, they constantly diverged into
dark and lonesome beds, where a continual gloom
brooded. It was in vain that, after our old fashion, we flung ourselves on the shores of the East,
and talked of its gay bazaars, of the splendors of
the time of Haroun, of harems and golden palaces.
Black afreets continually arose from the depths of
our talk, and expanded, like the one the fisherman
released from the copper vessel, until they blotted
everything bright from our vision. Insensibly, we
yielded to the occult force that swayed us, and indulged in gloomy speculation. We had talked
some time upon the proneness of the human mind
to mysticism, and the almost universal love of the
terrible, when Hammond suddenly said to me,

"What do you consider to be the greatest element of terror?"

The question puzzled me. That many things were terrible, I knew. But it now struck me, for the first time, that there must be one great and ruling embodiment of fear—a King of Terrors, to which all others must succumb. What might it be? To what train of circumstances would it owe its existence?

"I confess, Hammond," I replied to my friend, "I never considered the subject before. That there must be one Something more terrible than any other thing, I feel. I cannot attempt, however, even the most vague definition."

"I am somewhat like you, Harry," he answered. "I feel my capacity to experience a terror greater than anything yet conceived by the human mind—something combining in fearful and unnatural amalgamation hitherto supposed incompatible elements. The calling of the voices in Brockden Brown's novel of 'Wieland' is awful; so is the picture of the Dweller on the Threshold, in Bulwer's 'Zanoni;' but," he added, shaking his head gloomily, "there is something more horrible still than these."

"Look here, Hammond," I rejoined, "let us drop this kind of talk, for Heaven's sake! We shall suffer for it, depend on it."

"I don't know what's the matter with me to-night," he replied, "but my brain is running upon all sorts of weird and awful thoughts. I feel as if I could write a story like Hoffman, to-night, if I were only master of a literary style."

"Well, if we are going to be Hoffmanesque in our talk, I'm off to bed. Opium and nightmares should never be brought together. How sultry it is! Good-night, Hammond."

"Good-night, Harry. Pleasant dreams to you."

"To you, gloomy wretch, afreets, ghouls, and enchanters."

We parted, and each sought his respective chamber. I undressed quickly and got into bed, taking with me, according to my usual custom, a book over which I generally read myself to sleep. I opened the volume as soon as I had laid my head upon the pillow, and instantly flung it to the other side of the room. It was Goudon's "History of Monsters,"—a curious French work, which I had lately imported from Paris, but which, in the state of mind I had then reached, was anything but an agreeable companion. I resolved to go to sleep at once; so, turning down my gas until nothing but a little blue point of light glimmered on the top of the tube, I composed myself to rest.

The room was in total darkness. The atom of gas that still remained alight did not illuminate a distance of three inches round the burner. I desperately drew my arm across my eyes, as if to shut out even the darkness and tried to think of nothing. It was in vain. The confounded themes touched on by Hammond in the garden kept obtruding themselves on my brain. I battled against them. I erected ramparts of would-be blankness of intellect to keep them out. They still crowded upon me. While I was lying still as a corpse, hoping that by a perfect physical inaction I should hasten mental repose, an awful incident occurred. A Something dropped, as it seemed, from the ceiling, plumb upon my chest, and the next instant I felt two bony hands encircling my throat, endeavoring to choke me.

I am no coward, and am possessed of considerable physical strength. The suddenness of the attack, instead of stunning me, strung every nerve to its highest tension. My body acted from instinct, before my brain had time to realize the terrors of my position. In an instant I wound two muscular arms around the creature, and squeezed it, with all the strength of despair, against my chest. In a few seconds the bony hands that had fastened on my throat loosened their hold, and I was free to breathe once more. Then commenced a struggle of awful intensity. Immersed in the most profound darkness, totally ignorant of the nature of the Thing by which I was so suddenly attacked, finding my grasp slipping every moment, by reason, it seemed to me, of the entire nakedness of my assailant, bitten with sharp teeth in the shoulder, neck, and chest, having every moment to protect my throat against a pair of sinewy, agile hands, which my utmost efforts could not confine—these were a combination of circumstances to combat which required all the strength, skill, and courage that I possessed.

At last, after a silent, deadly, exhausting struggle, I got my assailant under by a series of incredible efforts of strength. Once pinned, with my knee on what I made out to be its chest, I knew that I was victor. I rested for a moment to breathe. I heard the creature beneath me panting in the darkness, and felt the violent throbbing of a heart. It was apparently as exhausted as I was; that was one comfort. At this moment I remembered that I usually placed under my pillow, before going to bed, a large yellow silk pocket-handkerchief. I felt for it instantly; it was there. In a few seconds more I had, after a fashion, pinioned the creature's arms.

I now felt tolerably secure. There was nothing more to be done but to turn on the gas, and, having first seen what my midnight assailant was like, arouse the household. I will confess to being actuated by a certain pride in not giving the alarm before; I wished to make the capture alone and unaided.

Never losing my hold for an instant, I slipped from the bed to the floor, dragging my captive with me. I had but a few steps to make to reach the gas-burner; these I made with the greatest caution, holding the creature in a grip like a vice. At last I got within arm's length of the tiny speck of blue light which told me where the gas-burner lay. Quick as lightning I released my grasp with one hand and let on the full flood of light. Then I turned to look at my captive.

I cannot even attempt to give any definition of my sensations the instant after I turned on the gas. I suppose I must have shrieked with terror, for in less than a minute afterward my room was crowded with the inmates of the house. I shudder now as I think of that awful moment. *I saw nothing!* Yes; I had one arm firmly clasped round a breathing, panting, corporeal shape, my other hand gripped with all its strength a throat as warm, and apparently fleshly, as my own; and yet, with this living substance in my grasp, with its body pressed against my own, and all in the bright glare of a large jet of gas, I absolutely beheld nothing! Not even an outline—a vapor!

I do not, even at this hour, realize the situation in which I found myself. I cannot recall the astounding incident thoroughly. Imagination in vain tries to compass the awful paradox.

It breathed. I felt its warm breath upon my cheek. It struggled fiercely. It had hands. They clutched me. Its skin was smooth, like my own. There it lay, pressed close up against me, solid as stone—and yet utterly invisible!

I wonder that I did not faint or go mad on the instant. Some wonderful instinct must have sustained me; for absolutely, in place of loosening my hold on the terrible Enigma, I seemed to gain an additional strength in my moment of horror, and tightened my grasp with such wonderful force that I felt the creature shivering with agony.

Just then Hammond entered my room at the head of the household. As soon as he beheld my face— which, I suppose, must have been an awful sight to look at—he hastened forward, crying, "Great Heaven, what has happened?"

"Hammond! Hammond!" I cried, "come here. Oh, this is awful! I have been attacked in bed by something or other, which I have hold of; but I can't see it—I can't see it!"

Hammond, doubtless struck by the unfeigned horror expressed in my countenance, made one or two steps forward with an anxious yet puzzled expression. A very audible titter burst from the remainder of my visitors. This suppressed laughter made me furious. To laugh at a human being in my position! It was the worst species of cruelty.

Now, I can understand why the appearance of a man struggling violently, as it would seem, with an airy nothing, and calling for assistance against a vision, should have appeared ludicrous. *Then*, so great was my rage are against the mocking crowd that had I the power I would have stricken them dead where they stood.

"Hammond! Hammond!" I cried again, despairingly, "for God's sake come to me. I can hold the—the thing but a short while longer. It is overpowering me. Help me! Help me!"

"Harry," whispered Hammond, approaching me, "you have been smoking too much opium."

"I swear to you, Hammond, that this is no vision," I answered, in the same low tone. "Don't you see how it shakes my whole frame with its struggles? If you don't believe me convince yourself. Feel it—touch it."

Hammond advanced and laid his hand in the spot I indicated. A wild cry of horror burst from him. He had felt it!

In a moment he had discovered somewhere in my room a long piece of cord, and was the next instant winding it and knotting it about the body of the unseen being that I clasped in my arms.

"Harry," he said, in a hoarse, agitated voice, for, though he preserved his presence of mind, he was deeply moved, "Harry, it's all safe now. You may let go, old fellow, if you're tired. The Thing can't move."

I was utterly exhausted, and I gladly loosed my hold.

Hammond stood holding the ends of the cord, that bound the Invisible, twisted round his hand,

" BOTH OF US—CONQUERING OUR FEARFUL REPUGNANCE TO TOUCH
THE INVISIBLE CREATURE—LIFTED IT FROM THE GROUND, MAN-
ACLED AS IT WAS, AND TOOK IT TO MY BED."

while before him, self-supporting as it were, he beheld a rope laced and interlaced, and stretching tightly around a vacant space. I never saw a man look so thoroughly stricken with awe. Nevertheless his face expressed all the courage and determination which I knew him to possess. His lips, although white, were set firmly, and one could perceive at a glance that, although stricken with fear, he was not daunted.

The confusion that ensued among the guests of the house who were witnesses of this extraordinary scene between Hammond and myself—who beheld the pantomime of binding this struggling Something—who beheld me almost sinking from physical exhaustion when my task of jailer was over—the confusion and terror that took possession of the bystanders, when they saw all this, was beyond description. The weaker ones fled from the apartment. The few who remained clustered near the door and could not be induced to approach Hammond and his Charge. Still incredulity broke out through their terror. They had not the courage to satisfy themselves, and yet they doubted. It was in vain that I begged of some of the men to come near and convince themselves by touch of the existence in that room of a living being which was invisible. They were incredulous, but did not dare to undeceive themselves. How could a solid, living, breathing body be invisible, they asked. My reply was this. I gave a sign to Hammond, and both of us—conquering our fearful repugnance to touch the invisible creature—lifted it from the ground, manacled as it was, and took it to my bed. Its weight was about that of a boy of fourteen.

"Now, my friends," I said, as Hammond and myself held the creature suspended over the bed, "I can give you self-evident proof that here is a solid, ponderable body, which, nevertheless, you cannot see. Be good enough to watch the surface of the bed attentively."

I was astonished at my own courage in treating this strange event so calmly; but I had recovered from my first terror, and felt a sort of scientific pride in the affair, which dominated every other feeling.

The eyes of the bystanders were immediately fixed on my bed. At a given signal Hammond and I let the creature fall. There was the dull sound of a heavy body alighting on a soft mass. The timbers of the bed creaked. A deep impression marked itself distinctly on the pillow, and on the bed itself. The crowd who witnessed this gave a low cry, and rushed from the room. Hammond and I were left alone with our Mystery.

We remained silent for some time, listening to the low irregular breathing of the creature on the bed and watching the rustle of the bed-clothes as it impotently struggled to free itself from confinement. Then Hammond spoke.

"Harry, this is awful."

"Ay, awful."

"But not unaccountable."

"Not unaccountable! What do you mean? Such a thing has never occurred since the birth of the world. I know not what to think, Hammond. God grant that I am not mad and that this is not an insane fantasy!"

"Let us reason a little, Harry. Here is a solid

body which we touch but which we cannot see. The fact is so unusual that it strikes us with terror. Is there no parallel, though, for such a phenomenon? Take a piece of pure glass. It is tangible and transparent. A certain chemical coarseness is all that prevents its being so entirely transparent as to be totally invisible. It is not *theoretically impossible*, mind you, to make a glass which shall not reflect a single ray of light—a glass so pure and homogeneous in its atoms that the rays from the sun will pass through it as they do through the air, refracted but not reflected. We do not see the air, and yet we feel it."

"That's all very well, Hammond, but these are inanimate substances. Glass does not breathe, air does not breathe. This thing has a heart that palpitates—a will that moves it—lungs that play, and inspire and respire."

" You forget the phenomena of which we have so often heard of late," answered the doctor gravely. "At the meetings called 'spirit circles,' invisible hands have been thrust into the hands of those persons round the table—warm, fleshly hands that seemed to pulsate with mortal life."

"What? Do you think, then, that this thing is——"

" I don't know what it is," was the solemn reply; "but please the gods I will, with your assistance, thoroughly investigate it."

We watched together, smoking many pipes, all night long, by the bedside of the unearthly being that tossed and panted until it was apparently wearied out. Then we learned by the low, regular breathing that it slept.

The next morning the house was all astir. The boarders congregated on the landing outside my room, and Hammond and myself were lions. We had to answer a thousand questions as to the state of our extraordinary prisoner, for as yet not one person in the house except ourselves could be induced to set foot in the apartment.

The creature was awake. This was evidenced by the convulsive manner in which the bed-clothes were moved in its efforts to escape. There was something truly terrible in beholding, as it were, those second-hand indications of the terrible writhings and agonized struggles for liberty which themselves were invisible.

Hammond and myself had racked our brains during the long night to discover some means by which we might realize the shape and general appearance of the Enigma. As well as we could make out by passing our hands over the creature's form, its outlines and lineaments were human. There was a mouth; a round, smooth head without hair; a nose, which, however, was little elevated above the cheeks; and its hands and feet felt like those of a boy. At first we thought of placing the being on a smooth surface and tracing its outlines with chalk, as shoemakers trace the outline of the foot. This plan was given up as being of no value. Such an outline would give not the slightest idea of its conformation.

A happy thought struck me. We would take a cast of it in plaster-of-Paris. This would give us the solid figure, and satisfy all our wishes. But how to do it. The movements of the creature would disturb the setting of the plastic covering, and distort the mould. Another thought. Why not give it chloroform? It had respiratory organs —that was evident by its breathing. Once reduced to a state of insensibility, we could do with it what we would. Doctor X—— was sent for; and after the worthy physician had recovered from the first shock of amazement, he proceeded to administer the chloroform. In three minutes afterward we were enabled to remove the fetters from the creature's body, and a modeller was busily engaged in covering the invisible form with the moist clay. In five minutes more we had a mould, and before evening a rough fac-simile of the Mystery. It was shaped like a man—distorted, uncouth, and horrible, but still a man. It was small, not over four feet and some inches in height, and its limbs revealed a muscular development that was unparalleled. Its face surpassed in hideousness anything I had ever seen. Gustave Doré, or Callot, or Tony Johannot, never conceived anything so horrible. There is a face in one of the latter's illustrations to *Un Voyage où il vous plaira*, which somewhat approaches the countenance of this creature, but does not equal it. It was the physiognomy of what I should fancy a ghoul might be. It looked as if it was capable of feeding on human flesh.

Having satisfied our curiosity, and bound every one in the house to secrecy, it became a question what was to be done with our Enigma? It was impossible that we should keep such a horror in our house; it was equally impossible that such an awful being should be let loose upon the world. I confess that I would have gladly voted for the creature's destruction. But who would shoulder the responsibility? Who would undertake the execution of this horrible semblance to a human being? Day after day this question was deliberated gravely. The boarders all left the house. Mrs. Moffat was in despair, and threatened Hammond and myself with all sorts of legal penalties if we did not remove the Horror. Our answer was, "We will go if you like, but we decline taking this creature with us. Remove it yourself if you please. It appeared in your house. On you the responsibility rests." To this there was, of course, no answer. Mrs. Moffat could not obtain for love or money a person who would even approach the Mystery.

At last it died. Hammond and I found it cold and stiff one morning in the bed. The heart had ceased to beat, the lungs to inspire. We hastened to bury it in the garden. It was a strange funeral, the dropping of that viewless corpse into the damp hole. The cast of its form I gave to Doctor X——, who keeps it in his museum in Tenth Street.

As I am on the eve of a long journey from which I may not return, I have drawn up this narrative of an event the most singular that has ever come to my knowledge.